## PRAISE FOR DIAMONDS AND DOOM

"Including realistic depictions of the Old West, life on a ranch, and the camaraderie of cowboys, this mystery is easy to read and hard to put down. One can't help but care about author John D. Nesbitt's point-of-view character, Rye, and his friendly partner for this novel, Dunbar. A master of building suspense quietly, Nesbitt has crafted a mystery and Western for a wide audience with *Diamonds and Doom*."

— *HISTORICAL NOVELS REVIEW*

"Nesbitt shuns action for characterizations and dialogue, tossing in a song and conversations about literature, not to mention vivid descriptions of Wyoming and a keen understanding of horses and the human condition."

— *ROUNDUP MAGAZINE*

# DIAMONDS AND DOOM

## ALSO BY JOHN D. NESBITT

*Western Short Story Showcase*

*West of Dancing Rock & Other Western Stories*

*Ridin' with the Pack*

*Ridin' with the Pack Volume Two*

*Ridin' with the Pack Volume Three*

*Across the Cheyenne River*

*Don't Be a Stranger*

*Justice at Redwillow*

*Boy from the Country*

*Twin Rivers*

*Silver Grass*

*One-Eyed Cowboy Wild*

*Great Lonesome*

*Coldwater Range*

*Wild Rose of Ruby Canyon*

*Bright Skies and Dark Horses*

### Jess Delaine Series

*Lost Canyon*

*Broken Horn*

*Forgotten Rose*

### Dunbar Series

*Dark Prairie*

*Death in Cantera*

*Destiny at Dry Camp*

*Dusk Along the Niobrara*

# DIAMONDS AND DOOM

DUNBAR
BOOK 5

JOHN D. NESBITT

**Diamonds and Doom**
Paperback Edition


Wolfpack Publishing
1707 E. Diana Street
Tampa, FL 33610

www.wolfpackpublishing.com



Paperback ISBN 979-8-89567-374-4
eBook ISBN 979-8-89567-373-7

*For my dear cousin Maryanne*

# DIAMONDS AND DOOM

# 1

The man named Dunbar came to our part of the country in the late autumn, a time of falling leaves, bare branches, and brief sunsets. A cold, drizzling rain had let up, and I was out gathering firewood about a quarter of a mile from the ranch headquarters. The fallen branches were dark on the top side from the rain, and I needed to fetch some pieces inside to dry. I was wearing leather gloves and breaking the deadfall into stove lengths when a rider appeared from the north.

He seemed to materialize out of the landscape, but I knew that was an illusion. Although the air was clear, the sky was overcast with somber grey clouds, and objects were indistinct at a distance. All in a moment, the rider became visible. The shape seemed to grow wider, then narrower, and wider again until it separated, and I saw that the man on the horse was leading a packhorse. As the party drew closer, I observed more details. The rider was a tall man wearing a dark, high-crowned hat, a canvas coat, and yellowish leather gloves. He was riding a blue roan and leading a buckskin. His horses' hooves did not make much noise on the damp ground. The animals were not breathing hard, and they did not seem weary. They were also not wet, so I imagined that the rider had found shelter during the rain and had come out as I did, when the weather let up.

With the lead rope easy in one hand and his reins in the other, the man brought the horses to a stop a few yards away. He had dark hair, eyes, and mustache, and his face had an open expression. He smiled and said, "I would guess there's a ranch hereabouts."

"Not far," I said. "It's called the Hook, named for the original owner. A man named Wes Galvin has it now. I work for him."

"That's good." The newcomer swung down from his horse and stepped in front of it, passing the lead rope around and taking it again in his right hand. Both horses knew their places.

I appreciated his manner. Some men will not take the trouble to dismount but will look down on another man for any length of time.

"What would be the prospects of a fella putting up for the night?" he asked.

He had something of a jaunty tone, and I felt myself rising to my best language as I answered. "Not bad, I think. I'm the bunkhouse cook, so I could invite you on my own vast authority, but we'll get the boss's approval anyway."

"A good way to do things," he said with a smile. He shifted the lead rope to his left hand and held out his right. "My name is J.R. Dunbar."

As we shook, both of us wearing gloves, I said, "My name is Edwin Ryerson, but I go by Rye."

"Can I help you with your work?"

"Oh, there's not much to it, and you look like you have your hands full. I can pick up this small armful and lead the way back to the bunkhouse. Not that you couldn't find it on your own."

He stood between the two horses, and I noticed that his hat and his coat were similar in color to the mane and the hide of the buckskin horse. I thought that at a distance, the similarity might have helped blur the images. Up close, everything was separate and clear.

"I'll be glad to walk along," he said. "Pleasant day."

The trees in back of me were dripping, and the clouds overhead were thick and grey, but the country around us was bare and quiet and peaceful. Knowing how the Wyoming wind could pick up in November and fling all manner of sleet and snow, I said, "It is at that."

---

I HAD a good fire blazing when Dunbar came in from putting his horses away. He hung his hat and coat on pegs, and he drew a chair away from the table to face the fire. The stove was a large, rounded, cast-iron model with a brass rail running around the base. I left the door open when I was building up the fire, and both heat and light came out of the opening.

"Good stove," said Dunbar. He sat up straight in his chair, a full-chested, broad-shouldered man. He wore a charcoal-colored vest over a tan cotton shirt with two pockets and a full row of buttons. I guessed his age at a little over thirty-five.

"Yes, it's a good one," I said. "The previous owners left it behind. It's one of those things you wouldn't want to move very many times."

"I like the foot rail."

"It makes a difference when the winter turns cold. Get your feet up off the floor but not too close to the heat. The boys like it. They should come trooping in before long."

The boss came in before the hired men. He hung his hat, nodded at Dunbar, and stood on the other side of the stove. The fire cast a glow on his wavy, reddish-blond hair. He did not have a mustache or side-whiskers, and his face was weathered like that of a man of forty who worked outside. He was slender with large hands, which he held out toward the fire. His blue-green eyes reflected the glow, and he did not seem to be troubled by anything.

"We've got a visitor," I said. "I took the liberty of telling him he could stay over, but of course–"

"Sure. It's fine."

Dunbar rose from his chair and held out his hand. "J.R. Dunbar."

"Wes Galvin. Have a seat."

"Thanks."

The boss raised his eyebrows as if the heat was reaching his face. "We're getting into the fall. We've finished roundup and shipped our beef. I usually keep one man for the winter, the one who's best with horses, but I haven't sent the boys home yet because I've got a little building project in mind."

"Oh."

The boss cast a glance over the newcomer. "How are you at that kind of work?"

Dunbar smiled. "I like it. The geometry as well as

the rest of it. But you could judge for yourself. I might be just another cowpuncher who thinks he can do carpentry because he can swing a hammer."

The boss laughed. "I've seen some of that. If you're not in a hurry to move along, I might be able to use another hand."

"That sounds all right."

"Stick around for a couple of days, then, and we'll see how it goes. We should be getting materials."

The room was growing darker with nightfall, so I used a twisted paper spill to light the lamp over the table.

The boss said, "Here's one now."

The door opened, and Kent Norland came in. He ducked his head and smiled as he took off his hat. He was a light-haired, blue-eyed fellow in his early twenties, of middle height and build. He was wearing a tan hat and a deerskin-colored canvas coat, and he had silver spurs the size of two-bit pieces. He had a way of making himself agreeable to others, so after he hung his hat and coat, he smiled and nodded to the boss and Dunbar again, each in turn.

"Evenin'," he said.

The other two returned the greeting. I introduced Dunbar to Norland.

"Good weather for ducks," said the young man. He took his place out of the way of the other two, near the back corner of the stove. "I had a teacher who used to say, 'Ducks on the pond,' but I can't remember what point he was making. Something about grammar." He glanced at Dunbar. "Good teacher, though."

Dunbar gave a light laugh. "Don't worry about me. I know my prepositions, but I don't hold anyone else to 'em."

"Yeah, we had to memorize 'em."

The door opened again, and Ned Hacker entered with a huff. He was shorter than average, wearing a wool cap with ear lugs and a coat of coarser brown wool with wooden buttons. He stamped his feet, shrugged off his coat, and pulled his cap from his head. His reddish-brown hair and ruddy complexion came into view. He was about the same age as Norland, but he had a rougher cut to him. He glanced around, and his gravelly voice sounded. "For a minute there, I thought I was the last one in."

"This is Dunbar," I said. "He's staying over."

"Ned Hacker." With his cap in one hand and his coat in the other, Hacker made no effort to shake hands. He gave the coat a shake, hung it on a peg, and stuck the cap on top. He found a place across from Norland, near the back of the stove, but he seemed to ignore his fellow ranch hand.

"Where's Tyler?" asked the boss.

"Don't know. Who fed?"

"I did," said Norland.

Although most of the seasonal work was done, the boss had the boys out checking cattle while they were still on the payroll. Norland, the first one in, had fed the horses. With silence in the air, he spoke again, in his cheerful tone.

"He'll be in. You know Tyler. Always lookin' after a horse."

Hacker still seemed to ignore him, but I did not know if it was about anything that had happened, as Hacker was surly a good part of the time.

I had cooked a pot of ham hocks and beans for the midday meal, and it was warming on the stove in the kitchen. I thought the oven was close to being hot enough, so I turned to leave the bunkhouse area and go to mix up some biscuits.

At that moment, the door scraped, and Tyler Hutchison stepped inside. He glanced around and said, "Hullo, boys." He stuffed his gloves into the pocket of his wool coat and unfastened the horn buttons. He took off the tan coat along with his broad-brimmed, dusty black hat, and he became a smaller-looking man of medium height and weight. His dark hair was matted down, and his brown eyes were observant but not critical.

"The other two horses must be yours," he said.

"That's right," said Dunbar, rising to shake hands. "My name's Dunbar. I hope I'm not taking your seat."

"Not at all. There's room for everyone. I'm Tyler, by the way." He turned toward the row of pegs.

"Anything to mention?" asked the boss.

Tyler's spurs jingled as he spoke over his shoulder. "Nothin' new."

Norland said, "Well, everyone's in for the evening. That's good."

As I turned again toward the kitchen, I thought I saw a scowl on Hacker's face. His eyes were not lifted toward Norland's but rather at the level of his yellow neckerchief. I did not know what to make of the expression, as the three young men were on an equal footing and as a general rule did not quibble among themselves.

"Everything's in good order," said Tyler. "And I've got a good horse picked out for you in the morning, Rye."

My stomach tensed, but I said, "That's good." I crossed into the kitchen and went to work on the biscuits.

---

DUNBAR WAS WASHING dishes at the end of the table near the stove. I stood by to dry them after they were rinsed. Tyler and Norland sat across from one another in the seats they had taken for the evening meal, and Ned Hacker sat a couple of seats to Tyler's right. The boss had gone to the ranch house.

Norland took out his watch and began winding it. His was an older key-wind and key-set silver watch, a kind that had been popular when I was growing up. I did not know if it was an heirloom or an antique he had bought, but I assumed it was valuable. He seemed to take pleasure in bringing it into view, fitting the key in the back, and winding. In addition to his yellow neckerchief, he wore blue wrist cuffs, so his performance had a bit of a flourish. Hacker, who did not carry a watch, looked on with an air of tolerance.

As Norland twisted the key, he told a story about a ranch cook whose clock ran too fast. He had the boys getting up earlier and earlier, so that even in midsummer, they had to wait more than an hour for first daylight. The boss had one of the hands take the clock to town and reset it at the train station.

"Turns out, his clock was almost two hours off. It took a lot of argument to convince him."

"Where was that?" asked Dunbar.

"Down by Sterling, Colorado. Not far from Nebraska, you know."

"Have you ever worked in Nebraska?"

"A little. For just a short while. Why do you ask?"

Dunbar set a handful of silverware into the rinse pan. "Sorry. It's a bad habit of mine. I like to know what work is like in other places, and I don't always ask my questions well. I'm either too general or too specific."

I said, "There's nothing wrong with wanting to know things."

"There shouldn't be," said Dunbar, "but it depends on what the things are."

Norland smiled in his bland way. "Work's about the same wherever you go. Depends on who you're working for."

I thought his comment was both inaccurate and self-contradictory, but I imagined he was trying to be agreeable. As he presented himself, he was not one to dig very deep into things.

---

TYLER HAD a horse saddled for me when I finished cleaning up the kitchen after breakfast and made my way to the barn. Sunlight was showing through the thin cloud cover, and Tyler was wearing a blanket-lined denim jacket as well as his black hat. The horse was a sorrel with a thin white blaze.

"We're gonna focus on one thing today," he said as he stood with the reins in his hand. "You said that other horse threw you right after you climbed on."

"That's right." I had reviewed the moment a thousand times, played it through my mind. With my foot in the stirrup and both hands on the saddle horn, I pulled myself up and swung my leg over the cantle. While I was suspended, with my mind not on anything, the horse bolted. He was a smaller horse, a very dark brown with a black mane and tail, running out from under me. I did not bail at once but rather bounced and slipped and jostled and then plunged, hitting the ground and skidding until I came to a stop with my head turned and my face scraped. My body smarted, but I was able to stand up and walk. The horse was waiting for me. I hobbled toward him, took him by the reins, and put him away.

I was in bed for several days, and I had a slow month after that until I was able to get around and work again. I had a great many conversations with the hired hands, and they supplied me with knowledge and wisdom about horses.

The little horse was devious. When he learned what my weakness was, he sprang his surprise. What I should have done was get right back on him and keep him under control. So they told me. But I had not had control when I hovered over the saddle, suspended in a moment that I always went back to in memory. As I explained it to Tyler when I met him, I had been spoiled by riding too many gentle horses that had always stood still for me.

"Today we're goin' to practice one thing," he said. "And that's gettin' on. This horse is plumb gentle, and he won't do anything to you, but all the same, you need to have him under control when you climb on."

He turned and put the reins around the horse's neck and settled them together on the right side of the saddle horn. "See this?" He pulled on the loose end of the near rein, and the horse turned its head toward us. "When his head is turned, he's not goin' to take off ahead. Don't let him walk out from under you."

Tyler tugged a little more and caused the horse to step back on its left front foot. As it did, Tyler put both hands on the saddle horn and his toe in the stirrup, and he swung right up.

"I'm sure it looks easier than it is," I said.

"We'll practice it." Tyler swung down. "A dozen times."

The nervousness returned to my stomach as I took the sorrel in hand. He was a sturdy one, larger than the little dark horse that had bedeviled me, but not more than sixteen hands. He was putting on his winter coat, so his reddish hair was soft and warm. I patted him and placed the reins as Tyler told me. Now I had to make a stretch, for I was not as limber as these young fellows who rode every day. I had to lift my left foot into the stirrup with my hand, keep my balance on my right foot, and strain to reach the reins and saddle horn.

"Now give a little tug."

I did, and as the horse turned his head and stepped back, I swung up and over and settled into the seat.

"Now don't let him move forward until you have the other stirrup. Make him back up if you want to."

"I see fellas mount up all the time when the horse is moving out."

"I know. But that's them."

We went through the routine another eleven times, and it was not always smooth and easy. But it averaged out, and I had the feel of how to keep at least a tame horse under control when I mounted up. I also had a sense of where my attention was. In the many times I relived the ill-fated moment with the dark horse, I could not remember what I was thinking of or seeing when I was halfway up and over.

"That's good for today," said Tyler. "How long has it been since you were on a horse?"

"A little over two years. It happened just before I turned sixty."

"That was before I came here. You're doin' fine."

---

THE BUNKHOUSE HANDS were going out to work one by one as I sat down to my own noon dinner. I paused to appreciate the aroma of the beef stew, and I became aware that Kent Norland was lingering. He stood across the table from me with his back to the door. I raised my eyes, and he put on a smile.

"I say, Rye, I'd like to ask if you wouldn't mind talking to me for a few minutes. Don't worry. It's nothing . . . disastrous."

"Well, I suppose so."

He drew out his watch and consulted it. "It shouldn't take long. Just a few minutes." He took a step toward the stove and turned back.

"Sit down," I said.

"I think I will." He put his watch away and sat in a chair next to the one across from me. He rested his forearms on the table. "Well, sir, as I think you know, I've had an interest in Vivian for a while now."

I do not think I controlled my facial features very well, but I tried to give no expression.

He went on. "And you being her uncle and all, and such an important person in her life—and, really, to all of us—I thought I would like to share some information with you. Before I talked to her, you know."

"Information?" I had an idea of what he might be getting at, and I had already felt a kick of resentment. But no one had to ask my permission, and I had told myself more than once that I had to let these young people live their lives, even if I thought my niece was a bit young and innocent to the ways of the world.

"Yes. Because nothing has happened yet. It's something I have in mind."

I could see that he was not asking my permission but more likely hoping for my approval. "Go ahead." I began to eat my stew before it went cold.

He took an object out of his vest pocket and laid it on the table. I saw that it was a brooch or pendant consisting of an emerald with a diamond mounted at the top. A thin gold chain ran through the clasp. The emerald was not large, perhaps half an inch long and three-eighths of an inch wide, but it had a deep shine. "That's pretty," I said.

"I want to give it to her. Or offer it to her."

I thought I had seen it before, but I wasn't sure where. "Do you mind if I ask where you . . . obtained it?"

"Not at all. I got it from Mr. George Marven. It belonged to Vivian's mother."

I felt as if I had swallowed a cold liquid metal. Vivian's mother was my sister. She had been married to a man named James Renfro, who was George Marven's nephew. My sister, Martha, died when Vivian was three years old, and Renfro died when she was about ten. She lived with a couple of other aunt-and-uncle families until she came of age, and she found work in Eminence, the town northeast of the Hook ranch. George Marven lived quite a ways away in the other direction, southeast of the ranch. I did not have an idea how Kent Norland came to know him or to wheedle this piece of jewelry from him, and I did not want to ask.

"That's very touching," I said.

"More than I can express." Norland poked at the thin chain and bunched it up by the diamond at the top of the arrangement. "I'm thinking of having it mounted on a ring, maybe with one or more diamonds as well, but I want to know if she'll accept it first."

"That's all up to you two," I said. "I don't meddle in these things."

"I didn't think you would, sir, but I wanted to let you know what I had in mind before I went any further."

I felt again that he was hoping I would express my goodwill or approval, but I was not going to give it to him. If anything, I was more appalled than before. "What matters," I said, "is what she thinks."

"Oh, yes. Of course." He put on his smile. "I want to thank you for taking the time to talk to me."

"You're welcome." I looked away for the tin plate of biscuits, and when my eyes came back, he had gathered up the pendant and put it away.

His voice raised as he stood up. "Well, I'd better move along and get after my work. Thanks again."

"You bet."

---

THE WEATHER HELD clear all day, and I spent the latter part of the short afternoon cutting up some thicker branches I had on the woodpile. I used a handsaw with a coarse cut, and it went through the dry elm wood quite well. Dunbar stopped to visit as the sun was dropping behind the hills in the west.

"You wouldn't mind if I carried in an armload today, would you?"

"No, I wouldn't."

A crow cawed from the peak of the barn roof.

Dunbar said, "The raven himself is hoarse."

"He sounds like it."

The crow flapped away, croaking, and settled into some bare trees a couple of hundred yards away and downhill.

Dunbar watched. "Light thickens, and the crow . . . makes wing to th' rooky wood." He smiled and said, "Sorry. Sometimes it seems as if the old play *Macbeth* is not very far away. Are you familiar with it?"

I imagined that both lines came from the play. "I've heard of it. I may have seen some little part of it, in a traveling show."

"Good stuff. Full of fate and doom." After a pause, he said, "I might not mention that sort of thing, but from the way you speak, you seem to be literate."

"I grew up in a house where we had books and magazines. Not a formal education, but I liked to read. I still do. You'll find other families in this part of the country like that, as well."

"Oh, I know. I didn't mean to assume otherwise."

---

THE PIECES OF ELM, which were four to five inches thick, burned clean and hot, and they made a good bed of coals. The boss and the four hired men took up different seats from the day before. Dunbar sat at a corner near the back of the stove, and Ned Hacker sat by the open door, where he could spit tobacco juice into the fire. He seemed again to ignore Kent Norland. I could not tell if their distance was deliberate on the part of either of them, but they had the full bulk of the stove between them. All of the men had lapsed into silence. Dunbar sat with his shoulders squared, at the edge of the lamplight. His dark grey vest reminded me of the chest of a buck deer, and he seemed to have an animal-like vigor or energy brimming within him. Across the stove at the opposite corner, Kent Norland sat as if he was waiting for church services to begin. Tyler Hutchison was seated between Norland and the boss, a little farther back from the stove, and he was braiding three leather laces together. The boss sat near the blaze with his large hands on his knees.

He sat up in his chair as he drew a breath. "Tomorrow's Saturday, boys. Work's not pressin', so you can have the day off. Good day to go to town. Dunbar, if you don't mind, you can ride along in the wagon with Rye. Pick up a few supplies. These young fellas want to get there quicker, I imagine."

Norland said, "I don't mind ridin' along with the wagon, Wes. You never know when somethin' might come up."

"Do as you wish," said the boss. "I plan to stay home and work on figures. Rye can bring me anything I need. There's not all that much in town for me. For you young fellas, it's different."

"Still no hurry," said Norland.

I lingered at the doorway that led to the kitchen. I had the impression that no one was paying particular attention to Norland, and I wondered if anyone had to make an effort to ignore him. I did not know if others thought, as I did, that he was trying too hard to make himself likeable.

I think that if I had had anyone to confide in, I would have expressed a sense that the way Norland was doing things with the pendant did not bode well. I think I would have said it at the time because I knew it was too easy to say such a thing later, in retrospect.

## 2

Our group of five arrived in town at a little after noon. Tyler had offered to ride along with the wagon as well, and so Ned Hacker had fallen in. The three younger men rode ahead of us in order to have less dust fall on their clean clothes. We parted company at the edge of town, the three riders going their separate ways as Dunbar and I rolled ahead in the wagon.

A large crow flew over, croaking, and settled on the peak of the livery stable. Dunbar and I both looked up.

"The raven," said Dunbar.

I drew the wagon to a stop at the post office, where I climbed down and went in for the mail. Among the half-dozen envelopes, most of them addressed to Wes Galvin, I noticed one that had my name written in unfamiliar handwriting. I put all the correspondence into the small canvas bag that we used for that purpose, and I went out to rejoin Dunbar.

"What do you think of going to the mercantile?" I asked.

"Sounds like an adventure. I'm always on the lookout for a larger sewing needle."

"Is that right?" I shook the reins, and the horses moved.

"In case I need to go to work sewing sacks in the wheat harvest."

"I think all of that work is done for the season."

"Oh, it was just a fanciful thing to say. But a fellow never knows if he might have to go back to work at some of the more basic jobs he has had."

"You fell into washing dishes well enough."

"That's part of being a cowpuncher. The same goes for sewing on buttons. I fall right into it. You wouldn't be surprised to know that I have my own little sewing kit."

I recalled the image of his packhorse, and I imagined the world of things that a man might have on him. "No, I wouldn't. But not all cowpunchers can sew on a button or mend a rip. They'll take it to town or try to have one of their pals do it. I can handle a needle and thread, but I won't do it for 'em. If I did, there would be no end to it."

"I agree. Unless it's something the work depends on. Like mending a cinch."

"Oh, of course." I brought the horses to a stop in front of the mercantile. "Here we are," I said.

Inside, we walked down the center aisle toward the counter. I kept an eye out for Vivian, but I did not see her right away. What I did see, with his head lifted as he stood behind the counter, was the proprietor, Raymond Fell.

He was a tall man in a dull black suit the color of burned-out firewood. He had a trimmed mustache and dark, wavy hair that reached his collar. He was slender, so his suit had an easy fit, with a white shirt, a crossed necktie, and a vest of the same black color. A silver watch chain glinted, and the steel buttons of his suit had a dull shine. Closer, I noticed his dark eyes, his prominent cheekbones, and his lean face with a narrow nose, the type that cowpunchers referred to as a hook nose and authors described as aquiline. He softened his face with an automatic smile and put his hands on the counter. He had good teeth and strong-looking hands, and I thought he could have been a dentist. But his forceful voice was that of a man selling goods.

"Good afternoon. I believe it's afternoon now. And how are you, Mr. Ryerson?"

I estimated his age at about thirty-five, and I assumed that his great courtesy with me was due in part to my age and in part to my being the uncle of his store clerk. He seemed to ignore Dunbar, but the presence of this outside person helped me feel, I believe, an artificial quality about the storekeeper.

"I'm quite well, thanks. And you?"

"Ready for what the day brings." He nodded to his left. "Getting my share of the news."

On the way in, I had noticed Thad Coulter sitting on a stool at the end of the counter. He was a portly man and such a common fixture in the mercantile that I had not paid him special attention. He gave a small wave of the hand that held a cigar.

"How-do?"

"Good afternoon," I said.

He wore a full suit, light-colored between tan and grey, with a flat-topped hat of the same color. He had a flushed face, light brown eyes, and a bushy brown mustache that was turning grey. He raised his cigar, but before putting it into his mouth, he raised an eyebrow in Dunbar's direction. "New man at the ranch?"

"Yes," I said. "His name is Dunbar." Gesturing with my hand, I said, "This is Raymond Fell, proprietor, and Thad Coulter, repository of knowledge about the town."

"Ha-ha." Coulter broke into a cough and overcame it. "You give me too much credit. I'm just an old man that can't do the work I used to." He turned to Dunbar. "When I was your age, I could do anything on the farm. I was a good one for stacking sacks of wheat all day long or hefting carcasses onto the meat hook. But those days are gone now. Give me a job where I have to lift something, and I'm as useless as a sack of hammers. Ha-ha-ha." He fell into another cough, stifled it, and pulled himself up with a whiffling breath through his nose.

Dunbar said, "I was just telling Rye that I've done a bit of work like that myself."

Coulter took a puff from his cigar. "You look like a range rider to me."

"I'm glad that I look like what I am."

"Ha-ha."

"Do you roll your own cigars?"

"Yes, I do."

"I thought so. It looks like you do neat work."

"Thanks. It's something I can still do."

"I imagine you have a good tool for cutting off the ends."

"Yes, I do. Like a little guillotine. Sharp."

Silence hung for a moment until Fell said "If you have a list, I can get Alan started on it." He raised his voice. "Alan."

The hired boy presented himself. He was about

eighteen, with wavy, light brown hair and grey eyes. He was something of a friend of Vivian's, so he and I got along well enough, but he was so intimidated by his boss that I did not show much friendship in the owner's presence.

"You can help Mr. Ryerson with the list."

Alan had his head bent forward. He looked up and gave a brief smile as he took the list from me. He moved away.

The proprietor reached into his jacket and drew out a cigarette case. It was made of dark blue leather and had the pattern of a diamond stitched on it with gold-colored thread. He opened it, took out a tailor-made cigarette, and tapped it on the case, then produced a long match from beneath the counter, struck it, lit his cigarette, and shook out the match. He turned his head and blew away a stream of smoke.

Coulter's voice rose out of the brief silence. "Well, here's the belle of the ball, the riverboat queen. What do you say, girl?"

I turned to see Vivian, who was standing where Alan had stood a minute earlier. Her face had a slight blush, but I think she was used to Thad Coulter's familiarity. She had never been the belle of any ball that I knew of, or on board any riverboat, so I felt that she found his exaggeration easy to smile away.

She directed her attention to me and said, "Hello, Uncle Rye. Saturday, isn't it?"

"Yes, it is. And good afternoon." I stepped back. "Vivian, this is Mr. Dunbar, a new hand at the ranch. Dunbar, this is my niece, Miss Vivian Renfro."

Dunbar took off his hat. "It's an honor to meet you."

"And the same to you." She gave him a pleasant

smile, and I did not sense anything flirtatious in her manner. She was eighteen years old and pretty in her own way, with wavy brown hair, blue eyes, rosy cheeks, and a trim figure that she did not show off, as she wore modest clothing as well as a salesclerk's apron. I imagined that Dunbar saw her as I did—not naive or simple but a young person moving into the world.

Dunbar spoke again. "I find it a great privilege to work with your uncle and to get to know him a little."

Her face had a shine of affection as she turned to me but still spoke to him. "You are a good judge of character, for he is a very good man. He looks after me without hovering over me."

"More people should be that fortunate," he said. "Most of the time, we're not able to choose our circumstances—at least, early in life."

At that moment, with all the attention on Vivian and Dunbar, I caught a glance at Raymond Fell, with his hand over the lower part of his face as he took a drag on his cigarette. His eyes were trained on Vivian in a way that sent a small jolt of alarm through me. He seemed not to be aware of anything else, and then in an instant his gaze relaxed. I heard my niece's voice.

"That's true. I believe I have been fortunate, in spite of some sad turns."

"Here's this," said Alan as he put a twenty-five-pound burlap sack of beans on the counter.

"Don't interrupt," said the storekeeper.

"I'm sorry."

"Don't quit working. Just quit talking." Fell lifted his cigarette with two fingers.

Vivian said, "I'll help him with the list. Excuse me." With a glance at Dunbar, she said, "Good to meet you."

"And the same to you."

Thad Coulter spoke up as I knew him to do, on an unrelated topic. "It's that time of year to hang a deer or antelope, isn't it?"

"Yes, it is," I said.

He took a long breath through his nose. "I remember the last one I shot. It was an antelope, running away from me at an angle, about six hundred yards. Got him with one shot."

I had heard the story before.

"Gave most of the meat to a poor family. Only so much a fella can eat by himself." He sniffed. "Now you, you've got a crew." He glanced at Dunbar. "You've got six to feed right now, haven't you?"

"That's right," I said.

"And don't worry if meat gets a little moldy on the outside in cold weather. That just means it's aging. It wipes off." He glanced at Fell, who was watching Alan set a slab of bacon on a sheet of brown paper. "Good use for the bacon grease. No money out of your pocket, really."

Fell reached forward to tip his ash beneath the counter. "I can't worry about something like that. I'm glad for the sales I make."

Coulter gave a huffing little laugh. "Well spoken. Like a man of business."

I moved my head to relax my neck, and I caught sight of something I had seen many times and often saw without thinking about it. On a shelf up above eye level sat a stuffed hawk with brown wings and a speckled chest. Its yellow glass eyes stared out toward the wall above the front door. As I recalled, the hawk had been on its perch when Fell bought the store a couple of years earlier.

I returned my gaze to the owner. Smoke was curling up from the cigarette in his left hand as he leaned on the counter and wrote on a receipt of sale. He looked up at me and smiled. "I do appreciate it, Mr. Ryerson."

---

As Dunbar and I drove away with the supplies in the wagon, I had a nagging sense left over from our time in the store.

I said, "Interesting chap, the store owner."

"I'd say so."

"He seems to like to get on my good side."

"Ingratiating."

"That's a word for it." The wagon creaked on. I said, "He makes me feel uncomfortable in other ways. I can't quite put my finger on it."

"Such as?"

"I don't quite know, but it's as if he wants something."

"Everyone wants something. I'm sorry. There I go again. It's not a very original observation, general as it is. But some people's wants are specific, while some are more general. Hard to tell about our storekeeper on the basis of one short visit, but, yes, he does seem to be on the lookout for more than selling bacon and beans."

"Everybody wants something," I said.

"Often more than one thing. Again, I don't want to seem as if I think I know all that much. But of the things you want, what's the first that comes to mind?"

I said, "I want to ride a horse again. I got banged up pretty bad two years ago in September, and I need to get my nerve back."

"Tyler seems like a good one for that purpose."

"He is." As the wagon lurched on, I turned to him and said, "What about you? What is one thing you want?"

He raised his eyebrows and tipped his head. "Oh, my wants are simple. I just want to be of use to any person whose interests I'm working for."

"Well spoken. Like a man of—"

"Like a cowpuncher. And a former sack-sewer."

I stopped at the saddle and shoe repair to pick up a pair of boots for Wes Galvin. When I stepped out into the street, Dunbar was standing by the near wagon horse, patting its shoulder. A woman and a child had stopped in the street in front of the horse.

I recognized the woman as a person who made her living about town. As common knowledge had it, the child was a little girl she had taken in. The woman was about thirty years old, dark in a subdued way, with a near-muddy complexion and shoulder-length dark brown hair. She wore a blanket-like shawl over a long dress with black and grey stripes. Her low-heeled shoes were scuffed. Her appearance suggested something like a French and Indian background to me, but I did not know her. I only knew of her. Her name came to me. *Madeline.*

The little girl was not quite dressed in rags, but she wore old, worn clothes and shoes that I guessed were secondhand. She had a mop of blondish-brown hair, but she had clean hands and a scrubbed face. I did not know her name.

As I drew near with the mended boots in my hand, the little girl looked up at Dunbar and said, "Is that your horse?"

"No," he answered. "I'm just looking out for him."

"He's pretty."

Dunbar patted the horse again. It was a stout bay with a star on its forehead. "Yes, he is."

"What's his name?"

"I call him Friend. What's yours?"

"Sophie. It's short for Sophronia."

The woman spoke. "That's enough. Don't be a trouble to people."

"No trouble," said Dunbar as he took off his hat.

The woman had kept her head lowered and had not looked at either of us until this moment. Her green eyes had a clear expression of courtesy. "Thank you." Drawing the child by the hand, she said, "Come on, Sophie."

I showed Dunbar the pair of boots.

"You weren't long," he said.

"Long enough for you to make friends."

"Not quite kindred spirits, but closer than some. There's less that separates us from them than from the very well off."

"Yes," I said. "And it's easy to have a soft spot for a little girl who likes horses, whether she's poor or not."

"Just a little *gamine*. They get lost in the city streets and swallowed up into the big, ugly world."

"Gameen?"

"Sorry. Something like an urchin. A child who plays in the streets. A girl child. The boy is a *gamin*."

"Where do you get words like that?"

He smiled. "From those ponderous sentimental novels that give us a picture of how others live. Who's the woman?"

"I don't know much about her. I've heard that her name is Madeline."

"Is she the guardian? They don't seem like mother and daughter."

"From what I understand, that's correct. The little girl is an orphan. Her mother was a woman of the streets and came to some bad end, and this woman has taken care of her."

"Sometimes the broadest outline of a story is enough. I would guess she makes a living of an unspecified nature."

"That would be a way to put it. I believe she does housecleaning as well."

Dunbar took a couple of quiet breaths as he gazed in the direction where the young woman and the child had gone. They were small figures now.

"What else is on your list?" he asked.

"I need to stop into the lumberyard and pick up a list of prices they were supposed to have ready. I can walk there if you don't mind staying here with the horses."

"I'll be happy to. If we have time after that, I wouldn't mind sampling some apple pie."

"I know where to find it."

---

THE SUN WAS SLIPPING in the west as Dunbar and I stepped out of the Arcade Hotel and into the cooling air. The clock in the lobby had shown the time to be a couple of minutes shy of half past four. A small crowd of seven or eight people had gathered in the street nearby.

"Must be time for the stage," I said.

"We could be like the others and see what it brings in. Here's our friend."

Thad Coulter was standing at the edge of the crowd with both hands on a tall cane. He raised his head and lifted a hand to wave at us.

Within a few minutes, the rumbling sound of the stagecoach carried on the thin air. Four horses came into view, pulling a coach through a low cloud of dust. The driver called to the horses as they slowed to a stop. He set the brake, held his cupped hand by his mouth, and hollered, "Eminence!"

The yellow wheels and undercarriage were spattered with dried mud, as was the lower part of the brown body of the coach. The vehicle creaked with motion, and the door opened. A bareheaded man with a lost expression on his face stood at the brink of the doorway with his hands behind him. The driver had climbed down from the box, and he helped the man step to the ground. Another man followed him, holding him by the arms. I saw that he was handcuffed.

The driver said, "You should have waited to let the others go first."

The man holding the prisoner said, "He needs to go somewhere before something happens."

"Oh." The driver stepped aside and looked at the ground. When the pair had passed by, he looked up and said, "Next."

A thickset woman in a man's suit and a woman's hat stepped down without accepting the driver's hand. She raised her head in the direction of the hotel and headed that way.

The next passenger was an attractive woman of about thirty or a little more. She wore a grey wool traveling coat and a matching cap, and her gloves matched the color of her black, buttoned shoes. She had dark hair tucked into the collar of her coat, dark eyes, a light but not pale complexion, and red lips. She did not head straight for the hotel but stood aside and looked up to the top of the coach where a man was bent over the luggage and untying straps.

"That's it," she said. "The dark bag. It has my name on it. Deville."

"This one?" He held up a black leather Gladstone.

"Yes."

The man held it down over the edge of the coach, and Dunbar moved in a quick motion to take it. "Allow me."

The woman stepped close and smiled as he handed the bag to her. "Thank you very much," she said as she lowered the bag to the ground.

"A pleasure." He swept off his hat. "Would you like me to carry it for you?"

"I think I can manage, but thank you."

He touched his hat to his leg as he smiled and said, "At your service."

I thought I saw a look pass between them, as if they knew each other. He did not appear rebuffed, and he did not watch her as she picked up her bag and walked toward the Arcade Hotel.

Thad Coulter made a half-turn and rocked from one side to the other as she passed him.

Dunbar said, "It's almost dark. We should join our friends before long."

"I don't know if I want to go," I said. "I'm not afraid of a saloon, but I don't like to put a damper on these young fellows out to have a good time."

"Oh, there's room for everybody. You said the next turn was yours, so I'll take you up on it."

I had let him pay for the pie and coffee, and the

evening was early yet, even though night was falling. "All right," I said.

The Double Eagle Saloon was a familiar place to me. It had a long bar with a polished wood top that shined from the brass lamps overhead. In back of the bar, two large pillars and a high shelf framed in a large mirror. On the shelf, a rigid golden eagle sat on a perch, and on each pillar, a small wooden frame held a double eagle gold coin under glass. Men's voices mixed from a half-dozen conversations, and music tinkled from the piano in the far corner. No women had appeared yet.

Dunbar and I paused halfway to the bar to find our young friends. Two of them, Ned Hacker and Tyler Hutchison, stood each with a foot on the rail and facing each other with a mug of beer in hand.

"There they are," I said. We made our way to join them.

I ordered four mugs and was pleased to take mine when it was handed to me. We were closer to the piano now, and a man was singing the verse in "Cowboy Jack" in which the lovers have a quarrel and Jackie rides away.

A voice exploded behind me. "Hey! What the hell! Can I get a whiskey here?"

I turned to see a man unknown to me. He was wearing a bowler hat and a black overcoat of coarse wool. He had rounded shoulders, heavy brows, and dark shadows under his eyes. His mouth hung open, and he moistened his lips with his tongue. When his drink came, he slapped down a quarter, took the glass with a twist of his hand, and tossed down the whiskey. He let out a long *Aahh!* and set the glass down hard on the bar top. He looked at me as if I was going to say something, but as he matched my idea of a perfect lout, I knew better. I returned to my company, and the stranger left.

I had drunk about half of my mug of beer when Kent Norland arrived. He had his hands in the pockets of his canvas coat, and he had the collar turned up. No one asked him where he had been, and he made no comment. He put on a smile, but it seemed to me as if he had to make an effort to do so. He had the air of a man who had just made a bad deal trading horses and wanted to put a good face on things. As I had bought a round for the others, I ordered him one as well.

His ready smile returned as he took the beer. "Thanks, Rye. I'll buy you one in a little while."

"No hurry. This is part of the first round, which is on me."

"I'm in the right place, then. Ha-ha."

The man had finished singing, so the voices of men talking went down a notch.

Tyler said, "Did you get all your errands done?"

I realized he was just making conversation. I wouldn't be in the saloon if I still had tasks to take care of. "Yes," I said. "I don't expect to stay out very late, but don't let me interrupt anything." I looked around at the three younger men. "Feel free to stay out as you wish and come back when you want. I'm not the boss anyway. We all know the way back."

No one said anything, which I took to mean that no one disagreed or felt an obligation to see the wagon home.

We stood in easy fellowship, the five of us, for another half hour or so. Dunbar bought the second round. Another man sang a song to the piano music, this one about a cowboy who has a fatal fall from a horse and gives away his saddle, spurs, and pistol before he dies.

When the song ended, Kent Norland said, "What kind of songs do you like, Dunbar?"

"I like 'em all, but I can get enough of the comical ones pretty soon, like the one about the Railroad Hotel. I can listen to the sad ones and not get tired of them."

"Do you sing any?"

"Oh, no. Not at all."

"Me neither. At least, when anyone's around."

Another man took a place at the bar where the lout had stood a while earlier. He was a tall man wearing a round, short-brimmed hat and a long, black overcoat. On second glance, I saw that he was Raymond Fell. He spoke to the bartender and waved at our group. A moment later, a round of drinks arrived.

We all thanked him, and he raised his glass of whiskey in salute.

I turned my back to him, and the next thing I knew, he was standing between me and Kent Norland.

"It's good to see you out having a good time, Mr. Ryerson." He nodded around to the younger men but was in a position to exclude Dunbar. "The rest of you, too." He put his hand on Norland's shoulder. "This is the time to enjoy life, when you're young and free. You get to my age, and you're all tied down with obligations."

Norland wore a tight smile and did not answer.

Ned Hacker's gravelly voice came out of his pink, scrubbed face. "You've got it about as good as anyone, don't you?"

Fell raised his eyebrows as if in surprise. "I suppose it depends on how you mean it. But I'm not young and fancy-free like you lads." He patted Norland on the shoulder again. "How does the song go? 'Once in the saddle, I used to go happy. Once in the saddle, I used to go free.' "

"Well, here's to you," said Hacker. He was wearing an almost-new black Stetson, and he tipped his head to one side as he reached his mug through the middle of the group and clinked against Fell's glass, which Fell had raised by reflex.

"It's a pleasant evening," I said. "Some of the amateurs have been singing songs of sorrow."

"Ah, yes," said Fell. He reached inside his jacket and brought out his cigarette case. He opened it and offered it around, still giving Dunbar the shoulder but at least motioning in that direction. I did not expect anyone to take a cigarette, and I do not think Fell did, either, but Hacker took one. Fell produced a long match, struck it on the back of his cigarette case, and lit their cigarettes.

He turned to Norland. "Don't smoke?"

"Hardly ever."

"Bad habit. Better to stay away from it."

Fell did not nurse his drink. When he finished, he took out his watch and said, "Well, I'd better be going." He smiled around. "I can't stay out late."

We all bid him good night, and he walked out without pausing at the door.

I exchanged glances with Dunbar. I would not have said anything even if I had had a clear idea.

Ned Hacker broke the silence. "Isn't he a good one? Half of us don't get a fair chance in this world, and some superior son of a bitch like him comes in and tells us how good we have it."

Tyler said, "That's just his way. Pay him no mind. Wouldn't you say so, Rye?"

I touched my tongue to my lips. "I don't want to say anything personal, but I think you're right. Try not to let other people's comments get under your skin." I thought Norland had more to complain about, but when I turned to include him, he was gone. "Where's Kent?" I asked.

Hacker said, "Prob'ly skipped out because he knew his turn was comin' up to buy a round."

Tyler said, "He might have gone to get something to eat. He doesn't like to drink too much at once."

"It's only beer," said Hacker. "But maybe he's delicate."

I stayed for one more beer myself. I told Dunbar I would be back in a little while, and I went out into the night.

The fresh air did me good as I walked to the boardinghouse. I did not think it was too late to call on my niece.

Her landlady, Mrs. Williams, answered the door and let me in. I was relieved to see a mantel clock on a shelf showing a few minutes before eight. I stood by an enamel-coated coal-burning stove as Mrs. Williams went for Vivian.

"Good evening, Uncle Rye," she said as she walked into the room. "I thought you might have gone to the ranch by now."

"I'll go before long, I think. I left Mr. Dunbar at the saloon, and we'll go back together."

Vivian drew her brows together, but the blush was still on her cheeks. "Is there something you want to talk about?"

I saw that Mrs. Williams had left us alone. "I

believe so. There's something that's been bothering me since earlier in the day, and I hope you don't think I'm too forward in bringing it up."

"Not at all. Here. Let's sit down where we can talk in quiet." She pointed out an armchair for me and took a seat on the couch that sat close to it.

"I'll try not to make this very long."

"Don't worry. Just go ahead."

I took in a breath. "You don't have to answer anything you don't want to, but I feel that I have to tell you that I'm concerned about whether someone is paying you more attention than you care for. And I don't mean Kent Norland. I'm not worried about him."

She gave a faint smile and waved her hand. "No, let's not worry about him."

"Anyone else, then?"

She made a circle of her mouth and blew out a short breath. "I suppose this qualifies. His fellow ranch hand, Ned Hacker, buzzes around me when he gets a chance. I try to brush him off, but he doesn't want to take a hint."

I coughed and had to regain my breath. "Ned Hacker? I don't suppose I should be surprised. And I don't mean that about you. Just about him. He has seemed, shall I say, resentful of late, and I didn't know what to make of it." I scratched my chin. "Is he any trouble to you?"

"Not really. More of a bother, is all."

"That's good." I paused for a moment. "Is there anyone else, maybe someone who is a little more subtle, or—?"

She grimaced as she looked at her hands in her lap. Some of the color had faded from her cheeks.

"Again, I don't want to cause any discomfort—"

"No, it's all right. And you're on the right track, I think. Someone more subtle and . . . furtive. But given who he is, it's hard for me to speak out about it."

Lowering my voice more than before, I said, "Because he has authority over you."

"That's right," she said. Her eyes were moist as she looked up. "He gives me the most uncomfortable feeling. He puts me in situations in which I have to talk to him as I work. He watches my hands, and he watches my mouth, and I feel as if he's trying to . . . take possession of me, even though he hasn't touched me—yet."

I felt as if the wind had been knocked out of me. I took in a breath and said, "Let's think about what we can do—nothing too abrupt, to cause any unwanted reaction. But if we can ease you out of there—"

"That's a good thought. As you say, nothing too abrupt. I don't want someone following me."

"You think you can wait it out a little while, then?"

"I think so. It's not indefinite. And if things do get worse, I can walk away."

"Good. I'm glad I brought it up. We can talk about it again before long."

"Thank you. I'm glad you brought it up, too. I didn't know how to go about telling someone else." Her face relaxed. "Take care going home. I know you know the way, but—"

I was able to smile now. "Fear not. I'll have Mr. Dunbar with me."

"Oh, yes. So much the better."

# 3

A LOW CLOUD COVER HUNG OVER THE RANCH AND THE surrounding rangeland when I walked out on Sunday morning. We had seen some stars on the drive home the night before, but the clouds had closed in. The morning was not as cold as it might be under a clear sky, but the air felt thick and damp as I wandered along. I needed a short while to myself after reading the letter I had received with the mail in town, so I drew into my winter cap, overcoat, and gloves as I plodded through the gloom.

The letter informed me that a good friend had died. He was a year older than I was, and we had been friends for twenty-five years. He was a ranch foreman, and his work took him farther north, up into the northeastern part of Wyoming and later into Montana. Although he was married, he made better wages than I did and was able to save enough money, as he put it, to take his old bones to warmer places. His wife told me in her letter that he had had an abscess for a few years, which he did not want to tell his friends about. He had died in Arizona, sitting in the sunlight, with a Wyoming elk hide over his lap.

The letter had come unexpected, of course, but as I walked, I reasoned with myself that even though my friend's death was an isolated event, it was a normal occurrence in a stage of life when people around began to drop off. I took comfort in reflecting that he lived as long as he did and had as much chance at life as he did. Still, I found it hard to accept that such a lively person, always active and ready with an opinion as well, was gone. I had to make myself understand that he had not been well, that I should have seen it in his lined face and grey hair the last time I saw him; but I remembered him best as a brown-haired man in his prime, trotting into roundup camp on horseback and swinging down with his spurs jingling. I wished he could have lived longer, but at least he had a full chance, and he lived his life, as he put it, in the big wide open.

Even though the gloom of the day seemed to press me in, I had an awareness of being out in the big country where so much of life ran free. I counted myself lucky to live far from the crowds and the din of the city, where urchins wandered in the streets and people died in the gutter.

I wandered along the fence of the horse pasture, where the colors of the duns and sorrels and bays were dull on this sunless morning. A smaller object caught my eye, a grey shape with a dark spot and a smaller white speck. I recognized it as a wild goose, the kind that came down from Canada at this time of year. They came in V-shaped flocks, settling in the grain-fields at morning and night. But this one was by itself, on foot, walking along inside the fence.

A dark horse began to follow it. The goose stopped, lifted its wings without spreading them, and opened its mouth in a show of hissing. It wandered outside the fence and back in, at which time the horse lowered its head and began to chase the goose in a rocking-horse motion. The large bird turned, lifted its wings again in its threatening way, but did not flap. It retreated to the fence line and made its way under the bottom strand, where the horse came to a stop. The goose waddled on, safe for the time being. I wondered how long it would last in this country where eagles and coyotes became hungry in cold weather.

On my return, I met up with Dunbar. I did not recognize him at first, as he was wearing a winter cap and a dull brown coat of sackcloth. He also had on a pair of faded brown cotton gloves, which I imagined stayed with the coat.

"Are you all right?" he asked.

"Oh, yes."

He turned around and walked with me. "You seemed a bit morose after breakfast, and then I saw you walking away in the distance."

"I'm all right. I just needed a little time to myself."

"I understand. And I don't want to give the impression that I think you need looking after."

"That's fine. I don't mean to be sulky about it. But I received a letter yesterday, and I didn't have a chance to read it until this morning. It brought something of a dark cloud over me."

"I'm sorry to hear that."

"An old friend of mine died. He was my age, a year older, but it still came unexpected."

"There's no good time for news of that nature—unless, of course, the person is very old or in bad health. But even at that, the news is for those who are still alive."

"That's what my friend said. Life is for the living, so we should get on with it. But still—"

"What line of work was he in?"

"He was a ranch foreman. He loved working in the outdoors, and from what his wife said, he died in the sunshine."

"Not in a sickroom, or worse."

"That's right. And I suppose there's some consolation in being in a place like this when I got the news—out here, far from the city and the tents of the wicked."

"Far from the madding crowd," he said.

"I believe I recognize that. It's from a poem in a churchyard, isn't it?"

"Yes, and it's used as the title of a book by Thomas Hardy. He writes stories about remote places where people have dreary lives."

"I haven't heard of him, but it seems like a good day for it."

"Every day is a good day."

"For those who are alive."

"Yes, and even for those, I realize that what I just said is not always true. Quite to the contrary. People suffering in sickrooms, as I mentioned, or languishing in prison. And if you think about it, every day has something fatal in it for someone. That's just the way it is." After a moment, he said, "I may not be bringing as much cheer into the day as I should."

"You're doing fine. It's good to remember that there's always someone else who is having greater misfortune than we are."

———

The air had dried, but the clouds still formed a blanket to keep out the sunshine at midday. Tyler was standing by the corral with the sorrel horse on a halter and lead rope. The horse was not saddled, so its full, reddish coat showed in the dull daylight.

Tyler was wearing his black hat and lined denim jacket. He tipped his head up as I approached. "I thought we'd back up and start from the beginning. Work on the ground."

"Whatever you think."

"Of course, the first thing you've got to do is catch the horse and put a headstall or a neck rope on him. I've got that much done, but we'll let you do that, too, in a little while. You're not afraid of this horse, are you?"

I shook my head. "Oh, no. I was on him a dozen times the other day, and he felt steady every time. No shake or shiver to him."

"That's good. A horse can tell if a man's scared. He can feel it in his hands, he can feel it in his legs."

"The horse that threw me was like that. He ran away with me a couple of times before the day he went out from under me. I would be riding along, and I'd think, what would I do if this horse took off on me, and he would do just that, until I reined him in. It was as if I telegraphed to him."

"Something like that. They say that a horse can smell fear. Maybe he can. Of course, there are some horses that even the best riders are afraid of. They wear gloves so the horse won't feel it when they're handling it. You know what I mean when I say some horses like to see how far they can go with you—or against you."

"You're right about that. I've seen some of it." In

truth, I had seen quite a bit of it. I have gotten rope burns from horses that were hard to catch and hold. I have dealt with horses that broke ropes and halters when they were tied up. I have had horses challenge me by rearing up or striking the earth, and I have had them nip on my arm, push into my space, and step on my foot when I was brushing or saddling. I have had several resist the bit, and one or two have bucked off the blanket when I went for the saddle. I have had them hold stubborn when I wanted to inspect their hooves, and I have had them move away when I was trying to mount up. More than one has moved out ahead before I caught the other stirrup. Some have seen fit to rub me against a fence post or take me too close to thick or low-hanging branches. And these were all tame horses, not the kind that good riders had reason to be afraid of.

"You've got to show the horse who's boss."

"I've heard that." I had heard it so many times that I wondered why people still said it. But I also knew that people who knew a great deal about horses might think that a person like myself, who worked in a kitchen and had had a fall, could use more education.

"So we'll start with a couple of things not to do. Things that keep you from being the boss."

"All right."

"First off, don't pet your horse on the head. That's where some horses have been hit and where some just by instinct expect to be hit. Most of the horses you're goin' to work with have been handled by someone else, maybe been in other places and subject to other kinds of work. You don't know what. When you meet a horse, he's new to you, and it seems like everything starts there. In a way, it does."

"So you pat him on the neck or on the shoulder."

"If you want to. Just not on the head and not from in front. You raise your hand, and he wants to get away from you. Same thing with pulling him. Don't stand in front of him and face him and pull on the rope. When you face him, you're telling him to stand still or go back. When a horse has a rope on him, his first reaction is to pull back, sometimes for very little reason."

"I've seen that."

"I imagine you have. So when you want to lead him, give him a little slack and turn your back to him. Don't hold him too close. Here." Tyler handed me the rope.

I took it, and the first thing I had to do was keep from moving my hand up the rope toward his chin.

"Just turn your back on him and walk. Give him at least an arm's length of slack."

"How far should I walk him?"

"What do you think?"

"A dozen times around the yard?"

"That's not a bad number. Repetition, routine, consistency."

"What's this horse's name?"

"They call him Partner. He comes out of Kent's string, but the season's over, and the boss says we can use him as much as we want. He says he still feels bad about the little dark horse."

"That's in the past," I said. "At least that's where I'm trying to keep it."

---

THE TEMPERATURE DROPPED when the sun went down. Each time one of the hands went in or out of the bunkhouse, a draft of chilly air rolled in. I lit a lamp and got a fire going again in the big stove with the foot rail. I began with a pile of twigs and then branches, followed by some pieces about an inch thick. When I was sure I had a blaze, I put on some split pieces.

Dunbar and I were the only two in the bunkhouse at the time. He stood clear and let me do my work, and as usual he was observant. When I had the fire built, he moved a little closer to the open door, on my right and at a wide angle, and watched along with me as the flames took hold. I put my hands out to the warmth, and he did the same.

At that moment, I noticed something for the first time. Dunbar had a dark spot in the palm of his right hand, as if he had been burned there at some earlier time. The flickering light from the fire made it more visible than before, and I could see that it was not just a shadow. I shifted my eyes so as not to be seen staring at it, but he did not seem to make any effort either to show it or to not let it be seen. For a few seconds, I wondered how such a scar came to be there, for I knew that in colonial times, convicts brought to this country were branded in the hand so they could not return to England. I also knew that even in my time, slaves had been marked that way so they could be identified if they tried to run away. I wondered how a man like Dunbar would have such a mark, whether it came from working in a place like a blacksmith or wheelwright shop or whether it came from some ordeal. As soon as I had that thought, I brushed it away, reminding myself that until I had cause, it was none of my business.

Dunbar waved his left hand as he lowered his right, in no apparent hurry, as he said, "I appreciate the way you manage your firewood. I see you have it organized according to kind."

"Thanks. This is elm, this is cedar, and this is miscellaneous, like salvage lumber or things I'm not sure of. Or things I don't have much of, like ash or wild plum. I'm working on the elm right now because I have quite a bit of it. And some of it isn't that good. I don't think I should have to apologize for it, but some of these thicker, punky pieces, even though they make the stack bigger, don't do much. I have to build up a good fire, throw on some of the soft stuff, and toss on some more hard pieces."

"You don't have much pine."

"Hardly any. What I do have is cedar. Old fence posts as well as dead limbs and trunks I've brought in. Some fence posts are pitch pine, and you want to set that aside and use it in little splinters, to start a fire. One old post I cut up was heavy and dense, not aromatic inside like pitch pine or cedar. I split each length into four pieces, and it burned hot and clean without oily smoke or shooting out sparks. Good firewood, and then it was gone, and I never had much of an idea of where it came from or, as they say, what its antecedents were."

Dunbar said, "If it was an old post, it could have come from far away."

"That occurred to me as well. But I have probably gone on enough."

"It's all interesting, these various ways of managing small parts of life. You're a gatherer of firewood—among other things, of course. I wouldn't want to define you. But this is one thing you do. I knew a fellow who was a gatherer of stones. Brought them in with his donkey."

"When you said gatherer of stones, I thought of a man who used to pick up small, smooth stones in his pasture and put them in a bed or border around his house. What do you gather?"

Dunbar took on a thoughtful expression. "I don't stay in one place long enough, but if I did, I might be inclined to gather antlers."

"On the hoof, or where they've been shed and dropped?"

"Maybe both. I've found some nice antler beams just lying in the sagebrush and in the timber. And as for antlers gathered on the hoof, as you say, once a set grows past a forked horn on each side, you won't often find two sets alike."

"So you hunt. Like our friend Thad Coulter said, this is the time of year to hang a deer. What would you think if we found some time for that?"

"I'm not the boss, but as the old scouts like to say, meat's meat. And it saves on eating your own beef."

"Which not everyone does, but that's another story."

He did not make a comment, and for a moment I thought he might be a stock detective. He turned his left hand palm up and said, "In the original view of things, that is, as the Indians see it, nobody owns land. We just use it while we're on this earth. And no one owns the deer or the elk or the antelope or the buffalo. But the white man came in and killed off almost all the buffalo, and the people who used to live off those herds would look at these slow, fat cattle and think, why scour the country for the remaining buffalo? To me, it's like a good joke. But the white man has determined that he owns his cattle, so he has all his laws of ownership. At the same time, he thinks it's clever to eat someone else's beef. So people have different ideas of a good joke. But I've probably gone on enough as well."

"It's all interesting. Even ownership and possession."

"Which aren't always the same."

"I suppose not," I said. "I haven't thought that far into it."

He raised his left hand palm up again. "Just for an example, a man can own a horse, but he can't own a deer on the hoof. On the other hand, he can take possession of it."

I made a slow turn with my head as I gazed at him. "Like people. One person can't own another, not any more in this country, but one person can try to take possession of another, without taking the person's life."

"They do it both ways," he said. "And there's not a particle of humor in any of that."

I did not think he was becoming contentious, just expressing something he was serious about. At this point in my life, I had begun to accept the idea that people younger than I was might have more understanding about some aspects of life and human nature. In more specific areas, such as horses or guns or machines, it was easy to see that a young person, like Tyler, might have superior knowledge. But I was slower to concede that a younger person might have more wisdom about life. Dunbar was giving me practice in that aspect, and I was beginning to think that it was not all philosophy on his part. It might have something to do with his work.

His good humor returned when, as a way of changing the subject, I said, "Depending on the weather in the next few days, then, we might either sort beans or hunt deer."

He smiled and said, "In a good world, we can do both."

The door opened, and Ned Hacker stepped inside without closing the door behind him. No one had been sent out to work on this day, but each hand still had his chores, and Hacker was dressed in his rough cap and coat. He stood leaning forward as he unfastened his wooden buttons.

"Close the door," I said.

"Tyler's right behind me."

"Still no sign of Kent?"

"Not yet."

Tyler came in behind Hacker, closed the door, and stepped aside to take off his denim jacket. "Startin' to wonder," he said. "We did his chores."

"I wish I had thought of it," said Dunbar. "I would have helped."

Tyler waved his hand. "It wasn't much. There'll be work to do again tomorrow."

I said, "I don't like to worry without cause, or speculate about what someone else is up to, but this is quite a while for someone to drop out of sight. Did either of you see him again last night?"

Tyler took off his hat and shook his head. "No, we didn't. He didn't come back into the saloon."

Hacker finished hanging his cap and coat and pulled a chair around to the stove. He shook his head. "Nah."

Tyler said, "It's not like Kent just to disappear. It's one thing if he went off with one of them girls with feathers, but it doesn't seem like him at all not to come back to work. Don't you think, Ned?"

Hacker had taken out his clasp knife and was cleaning his nails. He shrugged. "I guess not."

Tyler raised his eyebrows as if a thought crossed his mind. "Maybe he didn't go off with a girl. Maybe he went to see someone else."

I sensed that he thought he might have said too much in front of me and was amending it. I said, "Even at that, he wouldn't have disappeared."

"Like I was sayin'. What do you think, Dunbar?" Tyler looked over his shoulder to listen as he hung up his hat and coat.

Dunbar shrugged. "I don't have any definite ideas. I haven't been here very long. On one hand, our young friend seems pretty sure of himself and is old enough to look out for himself. We don't want to worry for nothing, as Rye says. We know that from our devil-may-care friends who show up smiling after a couple of days and ask us what the hell there was to worry about. On the other hand, some people go missing for reasons they would have done anything to avoid. For someone who tends to his work and meets his responsibilities, as he seems to do, I wouldn't expect him to be gone long—of his own accord."

Tyler nodded in agreement. Ned Hacker did not give much evidence that he cared, but at least he was not showing false sympathy.

I spoke again. "When you say you wouldn't expect him to be gone long, what length of time would you have in mind?"

Dunbar looked around at all of us. "Not trying to make anyone worry, but not wanting to make light of it either, I would say, about as long as he has been gone."

# 4

Kent Norland's bunk was still empty on Monday morning. The boss sent Dunbar in his place to ride out with the other two to check cattle. Left to myself, I scrubbed my two large cast-iron skillets, put them on the top of the heating stove to dry, and greased the insides as the metal became hot. Thin black smoke was rising with the smell of bacon grease when I heard a knock on the front door of the bunkhouse. I crossed the room and opened the door. Standing in the weak sunlight, wrapped up in a long coat of dark-dyed rabbit fur and topped with a tan felt hat, was George Marven. He had his hands in his coat pockets.

I spoke in surprise. "Good morning, George. Come in out of the cold." Behind him, I saw a man sitting in the driver's seat of a buggy with a blanket over his lap.

"Thanks." Marven stamped his feet on the steps outside and again on the mat inside.

I closed the door. "Come on over to the stove," I said. "I've got a couple of skillets I need to put in the kitchen." I picked my cloth pad off the table, and I moved one shiny skillet and then the other to the top of the kitchen stove, which had cooled.

When I returned to my visitor, he had unbuttoned his overcoat. He was dressed in a clean, cream-colored wool shirt with a pale blue silk neck scarf. He wore light brown wool pants with grey pinstripes, and his brown boots were polished. He shifted his feet as he moved back from the stove a couple of inches. His face stretched as he held his hands low to the fire. His skin was pale from not going out much, and brown spots showed on the backs of his hands.

He raised his head to look at me, and his pale face, always clean-shaven, had reddish patches of broken skin that I recognized as common in older people. He was about ten years older than I was. His washed-out blue eyes held on me, and the wrinkles at his mouth moved.

"Edwin, I've come to talk about something that has me concerned."

I nodded. I understood that leaving his house was a significant act. He did not do much work on his place at this stage in life, and he did not have a reputation for being a devil of a worker when he was younger. In recent years, he leased out his farmland. He had a woman who came in to do the housework and a man who came by, also a few times a week, to move firewood and clean the stable. I assumed it was the same man who was sitting in the buggy, waiting.

"I'll be glad to listen to you," I said.

"It's about this young fellow who's been working for you here."

"Kent Norland."

"Yes. I understand he's gone missing."

"I didn't know it was news yet."

"I believe it came from one of your men yesterday."

I thought of Ned Hacker, who might have been out and talked to another rider in passing. "Could be. You know how news travels."

"Especially bad news."

I said, "We don't know that anything has happened to him. Not yet."

"He hasn't come in, though, has he?"

"Well, no, but that doesn't mean something has—"

"He could have taken off." Marven's voice had a sulky tone.

"I don't know if that's likely. His things are still here."

Marven shook his head. "I'm as put out at myself as anything else. I let him get on my good side, and he took advantage of me."

"Oh."

"Yes. You know, he's all sweet on Vivian. I guess he heard about me from her. He came and buttered me up, told me how important I was and how I was the grand old man of the family—not exactly his words—and he said he had heard that I had something that had belonged to Vivian's mother. Which I did. It was a brooch. James had given it to her, and when she died, he kept it as a memento, and when he died, it was among the things that came to me."

"I see."

"And he talked me out of it. Afterward, I could think back and see how he had done it, and I wasn't at all happy about it. But I couldn't take it back, and after all, he gave me to understand that Vivian was ready to accept it as a token of engagement."

"Really? She hadn't given me any indication of that."

"You know how young people are. It doesn't surprise me that you wouldn't know."

I had to catch my breath. It was as if he was boasting about knowing more than I did. "And so he ended up with this jewel."

"It's a brooch." He pronounced it with such a long *o* that he sounded like an old lady. "Quite distinctive, and it has some value. It's an emerald with a diamond above it, set on a gold clasp, with a thin gold chain. Quite appropriate for a young lady, as far as that goes, but I doubt that it has gotten that far."

"It didn't seem to, when I saw her on Saturday evening—which, as far as I know, was after anyone else had seen the young man in question."

Marven's head made a small side-to-side motion. The skin around his mouth moved, and he spoke again. "I believe the emerald is of high quality. I don't like the idea of this young fellow getting off with it. And then if something has happened to him, I don't like the idea of it falling into someone else's hands."

"I understand why you're concerned," I said, using his word from earlier.

He pursed his lips. "I'm telling you this in confidence, you know. This information has the most value if fewer people know about it, but it could lose its value if only one person knows. So I'm sharing it with you with the hope that you won't . . . divulge it to someone else unless there's a good reason. A very good reason. I'd like to say that I'm sharing it on that condition, but I've already told you, so I'm just saying that I hope you can keep it to yourself."

"I know how to be discreet," I said. "And for all we

know, Kent Norland could come walking in at any moment."

Marven spread his tight mouth in a matter-of-fact way. "How likely do you think that is?"

"In truth, not very. I don't have a good feeling about it."

"Neither do I." He took a pair of lined leather gloves from his coat pocket. "Well, Edwin, I've got to be going."

"Won't you stay for coffee? I can put on a pot."

"No, I need to get back to my place. I have too much to do."

"Very well." I followed him to the door and waited as his driver handed him up into the buggy and drove away.

Marven was the only one who still called me by my first name, and I felt as if he was patting me on the head as he did when I was six years old. But I understood where he was in life's journey, and I understood his being more concerned for the heirloom piece of jewelry than for the young man who had talked him out of it. And I had given him my word, in a way, which meant that I would not share my knowledge with Dunbar for the time being, even though Dunbar seemed to have at least a passing interest in Kent Norland.

---

THE WARMER PART of the afternoon was already slipping away when I found time to go to the corral. On an old brass saddle horn nailed to a corral post, I found a hackamore and mecate that Tyler said he would leave for me so that I could catch Partner on my own and take him out for a dozen rounds.

Tyler knew that I had been around horses enough to be able to catch a tame one, not to mention saddle one. What I needed was practice in handling and control, and I needed to build up to it. I knew a hackamore when I saw it, and the lead rope made of hemp or horsehair that was called a mecate—or, as Ned Hacker and others called it, a McCarty. I took the setup that Tyler had left me and went into the corral.

Partner walked back and forth, keeping his hip to me. I followed him and cut him off each time. I kept my eye on his neck and shoulder when he had his left side to me. Before long, I laid my right hand on his back, at the top of his ribs. I moved the rope and hackamore to that hand, and the horse stood still. I passed the headstall under his chin, brought it up around his nose, and fastened it. Still without making sudden motions, I draped the hemp mecate from the off side and caught it with my left hand. I turned my back to Partner and led him out of the corral.

As I brushed his coat and combed his mane and tail, I had no age. I was a boy with his horse, feeling his steady, warm body beneath my bare hand. Partner was all the good horses I had known—good, I realized, in my terms. For Tyler or Dunbar, a good horse was one that could turn fast and cut off a calf, or burst straight out and take off at full bore. A good horse to me was one that was not going to put his nose to his feet and throw me into a pile of rocks or cactus.

After a dozen rounds on foot, I brushed the horse again, although he had not worked up a sweat. I led him into the corral, turned him to face me, and slipped off the hackamore. I hung it and the mecate on the weathered saddle horn and slid the latch on the gate. The shadows were growing long. I stood for a few moments, appreciating the time I had had with the horse.

Movement in a leafless elm tree some forty yards away caught my attention. A great horned owl settled on an open branch, and after a brief moment, he began to hoot in the haunting way owls have. He poised himself in a leaning, almost horizontal position instead of the roosting position I was accustomed to seeing. I wondered if he saw a small creature in the grass.

I held still. I did not want to disturb him, but he took flight. With slow beats of his wings, which were longer than I would have thought, he dipped and glided, past the corral and over a bare stretch of pasture. He came to a fluttering stop, a dark form now, in the bare trees downhill where the crow had settled a few days earlier.

———

I WAS outside gathering firewood from the woodpile the next morning after breakfast when commotion made me stand up and look around.

It was a familiar scene—a horse grunting and thumping as it arched its back, one man and then another shouting, the loose horse rocking and running away, and a man pushing himself up from the ground.

The thrown rider was Ned Hacker, bareheaded and flinging curses. Tyler Hutchison was walking his way.

From the hitching rail in front of the barn, a third man, wearing a black hat, Dunbar, pulled a grey horse around, sprang into the saddle, and went after the runaway horse.

In a moment, he was swinging his rope and leaning into the task. He gained on the other horse, which kept loping now that it was being pursued. Dunbar caught up with it on the left side, made his throw, and caught the horse. A few minutes later, he led it into the ranch yard.

Hacker had risen to his feet and was walking around, so I assumed I was not needed. I went into the bunkhouse and went to work on the midday meal.

---

The conversation at the end of noon dinner brought up the incident of the runaway horse, followed by a discussion of ropes, including what was the best for a given situation or a given kind of weather. The men spoke of lariats and how the leather needed to be oiled in cold weather, and they spoke of grass ropes and how they spoiled in wet weather and went stiff in damp, freezing weather. Dunbar said his rope was a maguey, which Hacker called a magee.

Beneath all their talk, I felt the presence of something unspoken, and that was the absence of Kent Norland. Dunbar did not speak much and was drinking a cup of coffee. Ned Hacker had rolled a cigarette, smoked it, and tossed the butt into the fire. Tyler was rotating his empty coffee cup, and Wes Galvin was looking at a little notebook that he carried in his shirt pocket.

The boss closed the notebook on the table in front of him, and with no introduction or transition, he said, "I wonder where in the hell Kent is."

Ned Hacker, in his gravelly voice, said, "No tellin'."

"Well, among other things, he was riding a ranch horse. That's not the most important thing in the world as far as what might have happened, but it's something to keep an eye out for."

Tyler said, "If it was on its own, I think it would come back here."

"That's what I think," said the boss. "But I guess we just wait and see."

"We could go out and look," said Hacker.

The boss frowned. "There's a lot of country out there. We wouldn't know where to start. We don't know where he was last. If he had been out riding in a certain area, we could go there. Sometimes if a fella gets thrown bad, that's how they find him."

I realized they were talking about looking for the body and not the horse. The boss had said they could wait to see if the horse came in.

"Just a suggestion," said Dunbar, "but Rye has talked about going out to look for a deer. Two or more of us could do that, and we could keep an eye out for a horse or a man while we were at it. Find a good high spot to begin with. This country isn't as flat as it seems."

"That's an idea," said the boss. "We can always use the meat, and it's good weather for it." He looked at me. "Do you want to hunt?"

"I wouldn't mind going along," I said.

"I think you might want to go up to Vaughn Butte. You have a good view from up on top, and there's deer down in some of those breaks. All four of you can go. If you want to go this afternoon, it's a long ways in the wagon."

"I can ride," I said.

"Oh. That would be all right."

---

WE REACHED the top of the butte at about three in the afternoon, none too early, but the day was clear enough that we could see for miles around. Nothing irregular presented itself, and we had kept an eye out all the way. Hacker had shown the most attention, I thought, tightening his face and giving a hard look to each side as his horse jogged along. I kept a lookout as well, but I also paid plenty of attention to Partner. He had a smooth walk and a calm disposition, and he didn't spook at little things such as when a jackrabbit jumped up out of the sagebrush.

A light breeze came from the northwest as we rested on the high spot. I began to feel a chill after a few minutes. "I think we should get started," I said.

"What's our plan?" said Tyler.

Hacker's voice came out of his throat. "Look for deer."

"Yes," I said, "but these things don't work well if every man just hunts for himself. One fella gets out ahead of the others and pushes all the deer away. I've hunted this place and others like it. The best way to do it is to have one man on each ridge and one man in the draw. They all go down at about the same rate, keep an eye on one another if they can. Pace it so you get to the bottom in about an hour."

"Everyone goes on foot?" said Dunbar. "Just to be sure."

"Oh, yes. One of us can take the horses around, stay out of the way, and meet the others at the bottom."

"I can do that," Tyler said.

Dunbar raised his hand. "I'll go down into the draw."

I said, "You'll have the least chance at getting a shot. The trees are thick, and it's hard not to make noise."

"That's all right with me."

I met Hacker's brown eyes and ruddy face. "Which side do you want?"

He pointed backward with his thumb. "The right side is good enough for me."

"Then I'll take the left. You should be in a good position. You won't be aiming into the sun."

"Anything I shouldn't shoot at?"

"Judge for yourself. Something with antlers is best."

"I assumed that. I don't know if I want to shoot at some little spike."

"That's up to you. It's tender meat."

"Less of it."

"Depends on where you shoot it."

He shrugged. "I'll see what comes up. Maybe nothin'."

I handed my reins to Tyler and pulled my rifle from the scabbard. It was a Spencer .38 that I had used quite a bit and had confidence in. I had checked it at the ranch to see that it did not have a live shell in the chamber, and I checked it again now.

Tyler took the reins of the other horses, and we went our separate ways. Dunbar waited until I reached the ridge on the left, and he began to make his way into the draw. Hacker had already wandered about a hundred yards down on his side, and I wondered if he was going to throw things off. I knew he was impatient and could get out ahead, just as I had warned against.

As I worked my way down the ridge with my rifle in my hands, I went in and out of tree cover. Hacker did the same. Most of the trees were cedar, with a box elder, now out of leaf, and an occasional pine. From time to time, I heard sounds from Dunbar's movements, which did not trouble me, as the man in the bottom was supposed to flush the deer out to the others. I made as little noise as I could, and I assumed Hacker was doing the same.

Sunlight still showed, but the air was turning cooler. I thought that some deer might be out feeding already, and I wondered if Tyler would make it around to the bottom in time to catch something that ran out that way. If we had had more time, we could have given him a head start.

I was thinking of these things and more when a rifle blast rippled across the draw. I held still, and two more shots crashed through the air. A minute later, Hacker's voice sounded.

"I got him."

I sidestepped down the ridge to the bottom of the draw, careful not to slip on grass or a loose rock. I went around a stand of chokecherry bushes and followed a thin trail through the buckbrush up onto the other side. I paused to catch my breath, then climbed the rest of the way up to a place where the ridge leveled across. About thirty-five yards away, Dunbar and Hacker stood looking at a deer lying on its side.

As I approached, I saw an antler sticking up. Closer, I counted three points on the right side—a fork and a longer tine. It was a mule deer, or blacktail as some called it, neither large nor small. Blood had leaked out of the grey-and-brown rib area onto the lighter-colored underside.

"Meat on the ground," I said.

Hacker tipped his head back. "I shot him, an' he froze still. I had to shoot him two more times to put him down."

In my experience, that was how a gutshot animal acted. If one was shot through the heart or lungs and didn't keel right over, it often ran for fifty yards or more and then dropped.

I said, "I'll hold a leg if you want, and Dunbar can hold the other—that is, if you want to clean him."

Hacker had brought a sheath knife on his belt. As he reached for it, he spoke with a tone of self-confidence. "Oh, yeah. I'll gut him. Let me put my gun out of the way."

---

THE DEER LOIN was firm and cold when I trimmed a length of it from the hanging carcass at noon the next day. I sliced the strip crosswise into little steaks and put them to sputter in bacon grease in my two skillets. I had fried a mess of potatoes earlier and set them aside. I wanted to serve the deer meat hot out of the pan, when it was the best.

The four men had taken their seats and were passing around the platter of potatoes when hoofbeats sounded in the yard.

"Go ahead and stay put," I said. "I'll see who it is."

I opened the door and looked out to recognize the tall figure of Raymond Fell coming to a stop on what I thought was a livery stable horse and saddle.

"How do you do?" I called out. "Just in time for dinner."

"I didn't mean to be any trouble." He stood up in

the stirrups, and with something of a stiff motion, he swung his leg over and lowered himself to the ground.

"No trouble," I said, although I had the little deer steaks counted and thought the portions would come out even.

He tied his horse and came in. I closed the door behind him as he took off his hat and long black overcoat.

"Have a seat," said the boss.

Fell cast a glance around the table and took the chair on Galvin's left, closest to the stove and kitchen, where I would have sat. I put a plate and a knife and a fork in front of him, and I hurried to the kitchen to take the meat off the cookstove.

I served the steaks straight out of the skillet, three on each plate including mine, and I put the remaining two pieces on the platter with the potatoes. Hacker followed my movements, swept a glance at Fell, and settled into his meal.

Galvin spoke in a hospitable tone. "It's not every day we see you out here."

Fell paused in cutting his steak. "I came to see if there is anything I can do. To help find your missing man."

"I'm not sure what there is to do right now. I'm not sure he's missing, but I think so. He was riding a horse of mine, and we've been on the lookout to see if it turns up."

Fell had a somber expression as he nodded. He kept his attention on the boss and did not look across the table where Hacker, Dunbar, and I sat. "I'm concerned about him, all the same. I hope someone can learn of his whereabouts."

"So do I," said the boss.

Hacker said, "We keep an eye out wherever we go."

Fell flicked his eyes and returned to his own plate, where he cut off a small piece of meat. "That's good."

"We think the horse would come back here if it came to that."

"He might. You know your horses." Fell directed his attention to the boss again. "If there's some way I can help, I would be glad to."

"I don't know what that would be."

"Someone could send for a deputy. I would be willing to do that."

Galvin nodded.

"And if one came, maybe some of us could contribute to expenses—board and room—so he wouldn't come and go all in a day."

"I don't know how regular that is."

"I could find out. If it seems to be out of line, I won't mention it. But if it makes a difference—"

"I could go along with a little bit, I guess."

"Just an idea. But I'd like to see someone do something."

"Sure. If there's something wrong, we want to know about it."

The men went on with their meal without speaking much, which was the usual habit, as they saved most of their conversation for afterwards. Fell complimented my cooking and said the venison was excellent.

I saw that his plate was clean. "There are two pieces left," I said. "Let me give you one of them."

He held out his palm. "Oh, no. I couldn't."

"Please do. You're the guest today. And the other piece can go to Ned, who brought the animal to the ground."

Fell smiled, showing his teeth. "How good. It was a nice buck, I hope."

"Reg'lar," said Hacker.

Fell smiled again with his mouth closed and did not protest as I rose and served the remaining pieces of meat.

When everyone had finished eating, Tyler told me to keep my seat and he would clear the table. Dunbar stood up and helped him.

Fell took out his cigarette case, selected a cigarette, and closed the case. I noticed that he did not offer a cigarette to Hacker, who sat across the table from him. He brought out a long match, lit his cigarette, and shook out the match. After he blew the smoke away to the side, he rested his elbow on the table and his finger along the side of his hook nose. A few seconds later, he took his elbow off the table and sat up in his chair.

Turning his attention to Galvin, he said, "I trust that everything else is all right out here on the ranch."

"Good enough. We shipped our beef, you know."

"Uh-huh. The last time I talked to you, you were planning to put up another building."

"Still thinkin' about it."

"Well, whenever you're ready, I'll be glad to provide any materials you'd like to order through me. I get the best prices I can."

"Oh, I know. I just need to figure a couple of more things."

Fell flashed a smile. "Of course."

Hacker finished rolling a cigarette for himself and lit it. He opened the door of the stove, which did not have a fire going in it, and tossed the dead match inside. Fell leaned to one side as Hacker came close, and he returned to his upright position as Hacker sat down.

"Any more news from town?" said Galvin.

Fell shook his head. "Not that I can think of. I should be getting back. I've got good help, but I don't like to leave my business alone for too long."

When the hoofbeats of the horse faded away, Hacker spit a fleck of tobacco and said, "He doesn't change much, does he? Just as high and mighty as he is in town."

"Everyone's different," said the boss. "He's not used to everyone drinkin' out of the same canteen."

"I guess not. I don't like someone who thinks he's better than everyone else and tries to act like he's one of the boys. He doesn't fool me. Does he fool you, Tyler?"

"I don't know. If he did, I guess I wouldn't know it. But I know he had the wrong words to the song the other night when he was talkin' to Kent."

"What words was that?"

"The ones about once in the saddle."

"Oh, yeah. He might have rode a horse out here, but he don't know much about cowboys. Not in a pig's ass."

# 5

Dunbar went out with me to help gather deadfall branches after breakfast. The overcast weather had come in again, and the morning dampness lay on the ground and on the branches. I had brought a wheelbarrow along, so we were breaking the branches into stove lengths and stacking them to be wheeled to the bunkhouse. I did not mind the exertion of bending over, straightening up, and breaking the dead wood, as it kept me warm and limber.

In his cheerful way, Dunbar said, "I believe this might be something like gathering furze faggots on the heath."

"The heath?" I said.

"Yes. Egdon Heath. In Thomas Hardy's novels."

"Hardy? The one you mentioned the other day?"

"That's right. Thomas Hardy. He writes tragic stories set in the provinces. Fatalism, pessimism, sadness. Common people playing out their stories on a bleak landscape."

"The heath."

"Yes. Not to be confused with the blasted heath where the witches tease Macbeth with their prophecies—though either of them might come to mind in this weather." He stood up straight and smiled. " 'Hover through the fog and filthy air.' That's the witches speaking."

"I remember them, but I haven't read much of that kind of literature. We did read some sad things in school. I think everyone read *Evangeline* and *Uncle Tom's Cabin.*"

"Oh, yes. One wonders if Little Eva in *Uncle Tom's Cabin* was named after the French-Canadian heroine. Seems like it, as her full name is Evangeline, and both of their stories are sad and sentimental. Not the same as tragedy, of course."

"I guess not."

"Tragedy isn't just misfortune. It needs to have an element of responsibility. That's what makes Macbeth's story good. He brings himself down."

I thought he enjoyed talking about ideas as well as about things, and I thought he enjoyed playing with ideas as he played with common work. I did not think he was an aristocrat or a professor in disguise, but I could tell he was an intelligent person with some kind of an education who volunteered to do menial tasks like pick up dead branches. And while he was at it, he tossed out ideas to an average person like myself.

I said, "I don't know the story. I just know of it. Like I said the other day, I think I've seen some part of it in a show."

"I don't mean to carry on a one-sided conversation," he said. "There are more down-to-earth topics. Like the disappearance of our young friend."

"That seems to hang in the air all around us,

doesn't it? It even brought the storekeeper out. I'm not sure what to make of him."

"Neither am I. But I don't know him."

"We talked about him the other day, and I don't need to say the same thing over again. It was no surprise that he was so cordial with the boss. But he seems to ignore you."

"He doesn't know me. And I don't have anything he wants. Neither does Ned Hacker."

His comment caught me off guard, and as I was bending over in the cold air, I coughed as I laughed. "At least you don't antagonize him," I said.

"Not that I know of. Yet."

---

Sunlight was breaking through by late morning. I was caught up with my work and had an apple pie in the oven, so I decided to sit against the sunny side of the bunkhouse and take in some of the sun's benefits. People said that sunshine was good for a person's health, and I believed it. So I took a sturdy knife and a stick I wanted to work on, and I sat in a chair facing the sun.

The stick was a chokecherry trunk I had cut about a year earlier and left to dry. It was about five feet long and almost two inches thick. I wanted to trim it into a walking stick. I started on the bark, which was smooth like skin and very hard. It did not come off in long strips as with greener wood, but if I had taken the bark off earlier, the wood would have split. I knew that from experience. So I had to do it the hard way, cutting off the outer layer in chips and small shavings. The next layer was reddish-brown, soft and powdery, and below that, showing through in patches, the wood had a light, creamy color. In some places, the knife cut down to the softer-grained wood, while in others, it skipped over the hard skin. I went to the barn, where the four men were building sawhorses and ladders out of old lumber. I borrowed a hoof rasp, and when I put it to work, it added to all the other wood fragments on my lap and at my feet.

As I worked, I recalled the old riddle about the creature that walks on four legs in the morning, two legs at midday, and three legs in the afternoon or evening. The answer was man. I did not consider myself to be in the evening of life yet, but I was aware of being an older man bundled in a coat, sitting in the sun. My purpose in trimming the walking stick was to have it for walking on steep or loose trails or for keeping a snake away. Perhaps someday I would use it to push myself up from my seat by the fire, but I hoped that day was still a ways off.

I was taking foot-long strokes with the rasp when I noticed a man on horseback riding into the yard at a fast walk. I did not recognize him, so I paused in my work and watched him as he came toward me. Although the air had been damp, the ground was hard, and the hoofbeats made a *clip-clop* sound.

I did not recognize the horse, a solid grey with a dark mane and tail. It snuffled as the rider came to a stop a few yards away. The man wore a light brown hat with a curled brim, a blanket-lined canvas coat, and plain leather gloves. He looked down at me and said, "Good morning."

"The same to you," I said. "What can I help you with?"

"I'd like to ask some questions." He pushed up on

the saddle horn with both hands, swung his leg over, and settled to the ground with a heaving breath. He was not old or heavy, so I imagined he was stiff from his ride.

He turned to me and showed a soft, pale face with a recessed chin. He had mouse-colored hair and thin side-whiskers. He was of average height, so he did not look down on me by very much as he narrowed his small brown eyes at me.

"I'm Deputy Caryl. That's spelled C-A-R-Y-L. People see it written, they think it's Carl. They don't see it written but just hear it, they think it's Carol, like a woman's name. So I spell it."

"My name's Ryerson. I'm the cook here. Everyone calls me Rye."

"Good to meet you," he said. He did not offer to shake, as he stayed put with his reins in his right hand. "Like I said, I'd like to ask a few questions. I understand that a fellow who worked here, Kent Norland, has gone missing. What can you tell me?"

I could see that he was not wasting time. I said, "Well, to begin with, his belongings are still here. So if he is still in the land of the living, he may or may not still work here, depending on what his story is and what the boss thinks of it."

"When did you see him last?"

"On Saturday evening. At around seven-thirty, as I recall. We were all together in the saloon, and when I looked around, he was gone."

"Who else was there?"

"The other three hands who work here. No one saw where he went."

"He rode a horse into town. Do you know what it looked like?"

"It was a horse from the ranch here. As I recall, it was a light brown with no markings. It would have his saddle on it, but I couldn't give you a detailed description of it. Nothing fancy or memorable, though."

"I see. Do you know of anyone who had anything against him or any reason to want something to happen to him?"

I shook my head. "He tried to make himself agreeable to anyone."

The deputy peered at me with his small brown eyes. "Who knew him the best?"

"That's hard to say. I don't know how well I know any given person, and I can't speak for anyone else."

"How about your niece?"

"You'd have to ask her."

"I did."

I had already found him humorless, and now I thought he was a bit self-satisfied. "Then you know more than I do."

"That's my job. And I need to find out more. Can you tell me where I might find your boss?"

"I saw him in the barn a little while ago."

"Thanks. And thanks for the other information you gave me."

"You're welcome. By the way, noon dinner isn't very far away. You're welcome to stay."

"I don't think I have time. But thanks."

"Maybe some other time."

"Always a possibility." He turned in a stiff motion and walked away, leading his horse toward the barn.

---

Ned Hacker sniffed out the apple pie and asked about it. I told him it was still cooling and would be ready for supper. I had already thought about how I would cut it into six pieces, and I imagined that Hacker might already be thinking about the leftover one.

Noon dinner consisted of deer meat, gravy, and biscuits. Dunbar volunteered to wash dishes. When the others had gone to the barn, he said, "That was a good meal. Good food for the kind of weather we've been having."

"The sun came out, but not for long."

"I've known people who live in cold, damp weather year-round. The women spend a great deal of time ironing clothes and sheets and other linen."

"I suppose they get used to that kind of weather. It's the world they live in. Here, it's just part of the year. But I've heard of places where it's bleak year-round."

"Reminds a person of Dickens. Bleak, like you say."

I waited for the rattle in the dishpan to subside. I said, "I tried Dickens one time and found him slow going. I think it was because I was pretty young. Someone thought I should read *Oliver Twist.*"

"Now there's one to go with some of that other sentimental stuff. But it's got other kinds of gloom as well." He laid a handful of silverware in the rinse water. "Dickens might have that effect on people, being slow, especially if they try to read him when they're too young."

"I suppose you've read some of him."

"Yes, I have. I read *Great Expectations* and *Bleak House* when I was old enough to appreciate them. I think I should read *Oliver Twist* again. I read it when I was pretty young myself, at the age when I might have asked for more gruel."

"I remember that part. It was dreary. All the boys in the workhouse."

"Picking apart oakum. Now that is real drudgery."

"What is it?"

"Picking apart rope fiber so it can be reused. Employment for prisoners. Punishment for sailors."

"Whew," I said. "Now there's a place where someone can get stuck in the fog and the weather. Ships at sea."

"There are some good stories about that," said Dunbar. "Though it's hard to tell which ones are true."

"About ships?"

"Ghost ships. Maybe you've heard the stories, and I don't want to bore you with the repetition."

"It doesn't sound familiar."

"Some stories seem to be more in the realm of legend than others. One of the famous ghost ship stories is about the *Jenny*. It's said to have been found near Antarctica in the early 1820s. Everyone on board ship was frozen, and the captain's last log entry was that he was the only one alive and had been without food for seventy-one days."

"I haven't heard that one."

"A more reliable story is about the *Octavius*, although the accounts vary and seem to be mixed with it as well. According to most accounts, the *Octavius* left England in 1761, I believe, sailed to China, took on new cargo, and tried to sail home through the Northwest Passage, which was not yet well known. It disappeared. Thirteen years later, a whaling ship near Greenland found a ship drifting and unmanned. Some of the whaling crew went aboard, and they found twenty-eight crewmen frozen to death. Farther in, they found the captain, a woman, and a boy—the captain of the *Octavius* had set sail with his wife and son—and they were all frozen to death as well. The whalers were all terrified, and they scrambled back to their ship, with just a few pages of the captain's log. Thinking that the ship was cursed, they let it drift away. This was in 1775. There's another version, from the same time, that has similar details but different names for the ship, but many of the details about the *Octavius* can be verified."

Dunbar had stopped washing dishes, and I noticed that his manner of speaking had climbed to a formal level, like a lecture.

"That's quite a story," I said.

"Yes. If you believe it, the *Octavius* traveled from Alaska to Greenland with a frozen captain and crew, over a period of thirteen years. A true ghost ship. One assumes it was locked in sea ice from time to time and drifted on."

"That's big and grand. People freeze to death here, but the stories are on a smaller scale. Someone gets caught in a blizzard while he's out checking cattle or hunting. A search party goes out after the storm, and they find him."

Dunbar was quick to amend. "Except in some cases. An avalanche, for example. A team of men sets out, in file, each one connected by a rope to the others. The search party comes back, but maybe they don't find everybody. Depending on where it is, they might find someone in the spring, but in the vast, frigid places, somebody might be buried in snow and ice for decades, moving through a glacier."

He resumed rattling dishes in the pan.

"All those stories seem far away," I said.

"Oh, yes. That's why we can talk about them in such a blithe way. A ghost ship drifts for thirteen years. Poetic."

I had an image of a lone deputy poking around on the autumn rangeland. "Not like our own story here."

"No," said Dunbar. "Not at all."

---

I WAS WALKING Partner with the hackamore and lead rope when a rider came galloping into the yard and stopped at the barn door. He swung to the ground as Ned Hacker pushed the door open and stepped outside. The two of them spoke in an energetic exchange for about a minute, and the newcomer sprang into the saddle and thundered away.

Hacker went into the barn and came out with a rope in his hand. He was taking fast, scuffing steps, and his face was more flushed than usual.

I stopped where our paths met. "What's going on?"

"The deppity found the horse, and they think he's located the body."

"Where?"

"Out by Swanson's place, just north of there."

"Are you going by yourself? Maybe someone else would like to go."

"They can catch up." Hacker leaned forward and marched past me.

Dunbar came out a minute later. "I thought you were here. I imagine you heard the news."

"Hacker's all in a hurry. Are you going, too?"

"The boss said we don't all have to go but someone

more than Ned should. I said I wouldn't mind. Do you want to go?"

I wavered. I had the horse in my hands, but I didn't know if I wanted to travel all that fast. "I don't want to hold anybody back."

"We'll let Ned take off, and we can go at our own pace. People hurry to get to a scene like that, and then they stand and gawk while the law takes all of its notes and measurements."

"All right," I said. "It would help if we had someone with a level head there."

Hacker came out of the corral at a fast walk. He had his rope across the neck of a brown horse with black socks. He handed me the rope and said, "Here. Hold this if you would."

He hurried into the barn and came out with a saddle, blanket, and bridle. He did a quick job of brushing the horse's back with his hand, then spreading on the blanket and slapping the saddle on top. Bending down, he caught the cinch while it was still swinging and ran the latigo through the ring twice. He pulled the cinch quick and tight, grabbed the bridle off the saddle horn, and pushed the bit into the horse's mouth as he held his forearm between the horse's ears. When the horse took the bit, Hacker pulled the ears through the headstall and gathered the reins.

He untied the rope from the horse's neck, dropped it on the ground, and set his reins. With both hands on the saddle horn, he gave a hop, stabbed the toe of his boot into the stirrup, and whipped up into the saddle.

"I'm gonna go see," he said, and the horse took off.

I picked up the rope, coiled it, and handed it to Dunbar. I still had Partner by the lead rope. I said, "I won't be quite that fast, but I'll have this fellow ready to go in a few minutes."

"I think I'll ride one of mine," he said. "I don't like them to get soft."

We had our horses saddled and bridled in a short while. I led Partner out into the clear, checked the cinch, and put the reins in place. I followed the routine I had rehearsed with Tyler, and with my mind clear, I pulled myself up and settled into the saddle. I held the horse still as I caught the other stirrup. The horse felt steady and calm beneath me.

Dunbar had his blue roan standing at attention. He had waited for me rather than mount up at the same time. "All set?"

I nodded.

He took the saddle horn with his left hand and stepped up into the saddle. "We're in no hurry," he said, "but we might want to go at more than a walk at least part of the way. How far is it?"

"About five miles or a little more. We go west and then north a ways."

"Past Vaughn Butte, where we went hunting."

"That's right."

I had not had to think much about riding the horse when we went out to hunt a couple of days earlier, as I had been in the company of other horses and riders, and we had kept to a fast walk all the way. "I think I can handle it if we lope for a half-mile or so at a time."

As I came to find out, Partner had a smooth lope. We varied from a faster pace to a slower one for about a half-mile at a time, and the horses were not breathing hard when we crested the last rise and saw the quiet scene below.

Ned Hacker and two other ranch hands who

looked familiar were standing in a loose group with their horses, the deputy's dark grey horse, and the light brown horse that Kent Norland had ridden. Ten yards away, what looked like a human form lay in the grass. A hundred yards out, Deputy Caryl was walking in a wide circle with his head bent toward the ground at his feet.

Dunbar and I let our horses walk down the slope. When we were within thirty yards, Ned Hacker raised his head toward us and spoke in his rough voice.

"It's him."

We rode another twenty yards, dismounted, and approached on foot. The afternoon shadows of the grass and low brush were beginning to stretch. The sky was hazy, and the shadows were dull as they touched the blond hair, yellow neckerchief, and deerskin-colored coat.

Hacker spoke again. "No sign of where he's been shot or stabbed. Not likely that he got throwed from his horse and has been here all this time. Someone woulda noticed."

Dunbar moved over to observe the body, but I did not have any inclination to see it in more detail.

"Where was the horse?" asked Dunbar.

"About a mile away. Took 'em a while to find the body. Deppity says it looks like someone took him out here in the night and left him, along with the horse."

Dunbar nodded. With his reins in his hand, he crouched facing the body and studied it for a long moment. His horse held back with a flared nostril and a wide eye. Dunbar rose to his feet and joined the rest of us.

"Sorry to see it," he said, "though I hardly knew him."

The deputy finished walking his circle and joined the group. After nodding to Dunbar and me, he said, "I don't think there's anything else to be seen here. It's getting late enough in the day that we should think about moving the body."

Dunbar turned to me, as if to let me speak.

I said, "We can take him to the ranch for the night. You can stay over if you'd like. In the morning, we can take him into town in the wagon."

Deputy Caryl was staring downward. He raised his head with an air of decision. "Might as well. I 'magine that horse will carry him one more time."

The subdued tone of our gathering was broken by Ned Hacker's voice. "You say you think someone took him out here and left him. Why do you think someone would do somethin' to him to begin with?"

The deputy shook his head. "I don't know. I searched the body, and I didn't find any personal items on him—no money, no knife, no watch, nothing."

Hacker kept at it. "Sounds like someone might have followed him out of town the other night and did him in for what he had on him."

The deputy shook his head. "He doesn't have any signs of violence on him—no bruises, no knife marks, no bullet wounds, no blood."

"Then you don't even know he was killed."

"No, I don't. Not yet. But when someone goes missing and turns up like this a few days later, it doesn't look good."

"How would they have done it, if there's no sign?"

"There are other ways that aren't evident right away—suffocation, chloroform."

One of the other punchers spoke up. "All of that for money and a watch."

"A watch?" said the deputy.

"Ned says he carried a watch he liked to show off."

The deputy turned to me as if I was a more reliable source. "Is that right?"

"Yes, he had a watch. An older key-wind model that some of us would recognize. Made of silver. We saw it a few times."

"Well, he doesn't have it on him now." The deputy glanced at the slipping sun. "We'd better get busy."

Dunbar stood by and watched as the deputy, Hacker, and another hand brought the horse into place and lifted the body onto it. The deputy then stood back with his hands on his hips as the other two tied down the load.

While the others were engaged, with comments here and there about where to throw a hitch or tie a knot, I held Partner's reins and appreciated his calm company. The breeze ruffled his red hair in the fading sunlight, and from time to time he let out a breath like a sigh. I wondered if he had an awareness that the man draped over the saddle used to ride him every few days.

I also wondered what thoughts, if any, the others had about this occurrence. The death of a young person is different from the death of an older person. When an old person dies, family and friends can take comfort in the idea that the deceased had a good life or at least had a full chance at it. A person has the sense that there is something inevitable or reasonable—even fair—about the passing. With the death of someone young, there is none of that. Nothing seems appropriate. Still, as I looked into myself, I had to be honest and admit that I did not have much feeling about the death of Kent Norland. I thought I should feel more than I did—that I should feel sadder. At the same time, I did have a clear sense that it was unfair.

---

UNDER LAMPLIGHT IN THE BUNKHOUSE, the deputy laid out Kent Norland's personal effects on the dead man's bunk.

I felt uneasy, guilty, about looking at his socks and underwear and razor and traveling mirror, along with things that must have been keepsakes—a piece of ivory with a rose etched into it, a small half-globe of clear glass, one half of a jack of diamonds card, and one half of the queen of hearts. Here we were, going through his private belongings, as his body lay under a canvas sheet in the bed of the wagon in the barn.

"Is that it?" asked the deputy.

"Nothing else here," I said. "This is the only place he would have had anything other than with his saddle or on his person."

"Well, that leaves his watch unaccounted for, any money he would have had on him, and I would assume a knife."

Tyler said, "He carried a pocketknife. Nothing fancy. It had brown wooden sides for a handle."

"You never know when something will turn up," said the deputy.

I had a moment of conscience. No one had mentioned the emerald-and-diamond pendant, which suggested to me that Kent Norland had not shown it to anyone else at the ranch. I had in mind my agreement with George Marven, that I would not mention it unless there seemed to be a very good reason. At the moment, I thought there was a good reason not to mention it. If anyone other than Vivian had it, it would be just as well if that person did not know that someone else knew about it. I did not think Ned Hacker had it, but I thought that if he knew about it, he would be all too happy to tell others what he knew. So I followed the line I had accepted with George Marven, that the fewer who knew about the jewel, the better.

Wes Galvin, who had been quiet all along, spoke to the deputy. "How long do you think he has been dead, then?"

The deputy pursed his lips and rubbed his small chin. "It's hard to tell in this cold weather, but I would say a few days."

"But not out there."

"No. As I told these boys, I think someone would have come across the horse at least."

Hacker said, "In that time, the scavengers would have gotten to him."

"That, too," said the deputy. He screwed his mouth to one side as he swept a glance over the bunk again. "I guess that's enough for now."

"I've got leftover meat, gravy, and biscuits for supper," I said. "I hope no one minds. On top of that, I've got an apple pie, and I plan to cut it into six pieces."

Dunbar, who had been standing at the edge, said "I'll help set the table."

As our little group broke up, Ned Hacker stood in place, watching the others. I did not suspect that he was thinking about the emerald. I thought he was counting to six.

# 6

DUNBAR AND I ROLLED INTO TOWN WITH THE WAGON IN late morning. The deputy had left ahead of us after breakfast, saying that he would have "them" expecting us and the body. By "them," I assumed he meant the barber, who received deceased people at the back door of his shop and prepared them for burial. I had not delivered a body there in the past, but I knew which door was his, so I found it with no trouble. The day being Friday, the barber was not as busy as he might have been on a Saturday, so we moved the covered remains of Kent Norland inside without interruption.

The barber was a slender man of average height with greying brown hair. His name was Jake Steck. He was talkative by nature, but for the present he spoke in a quiet, respectful tone as he repeated what I imagined was now common knowledge about where the body was found, how long the young man had been missing, and how he might have come to be there.

"It's such a pity," he said. "But we'll do the best for him."

I was thankful to be out in the cold, fresh air again as I drove the wagon around and stopped in front of the post office. I reached under the seat for the small canvas bag.

"I'll check on something while you're in there," said Dunbar. He waited for me to climb down and then did the same.

As the postmaster handed me the mail, I saw right away that none of the four envelopes had my name, so I felt a small sense of relief. I stacked the envelopes together and poked them into the open bag.

"Got 'im delivered, eh?" The postmaster could have passed for a brother of the barber, but his last name was Short. The post office was across the street from the barbershop, and the two places were such efficient centers of gossip that either of them was up to date with what went on in any of the alleys in town.

"Yes," I said as I pulled the drawstring on the bag.

"Too bad. Always had a good word when he came in here. Joked that he didn't ever get any love letters in the mail."

"I wouldn't know." I looked past him at a pendulum clock on the wall and saw that it was almost noon.

"Oh, it was just his way. We're all sorry to hear what happened."

"Thanks. So are we."

I waited outside by the wagon, not sure where the next stop would be. I had my list as always, but I had not decided on the sequence.

Dunbar appeared from beneath the awning of the Arcade Hotel, across the street and down a couple of doors to the right. He walked toward me and did not speak until he came to a stop.

"Do you remember the lady who came in on the coach the other day, Mrs. Deville?"

Her image appeared in my mind. "Oh, yes."

"She invites us to a small lunch."

His tone of familiarity confirmed my earlier impression that they knew each other. "The two of us?"

"Yes. She's interested in knowing a few people from here, and I told her she couldn't do any better than you."

"That's quite a compliment. You have me worried."

"I didn't mean to overdo it. I didn't think you would object, so I told her I thought she could count on us in about twenty minutes."

"Let me think of what that gives us time to do. Oh, yes. The boss asked me to pick up some camphor at the druggist's. It's just down the street. The druggist and the doctor are the same person. Is there anything you need there?"

"No. It would be interesting to know if anyone has bought chloroform in the last little while, but I would imagine that if someone had a use for such a thing, he wouldn't buy it here in town."

---

Mrs. Deville was waiting for us at a table in the far corner of the hotel dining room. With our hats in our hands, we walked past a table where Deputy Caryl was putting away a meal of sliced ham and scalloped potatoes. He looked up and nodded but paid us no more attention.

At Mrs. Deville's table, Dunbar introduced us to one another without speaking loud.

"I am glad you could join us," she said, also in a moderated tone. "Please sit down."

I took a chair with my back to the rest of the room. I was not superstitious that way, and I was sure Dunbar would not miss anything from his seat across from me.

I found Mrs. Deville likeable right away, with her clear, dark eyes and courteous expression. She had her dark hair pinned up, and she wore a midnight blue wool dress with full sleeves and a flat collar—rather businesslike, it seemed to me.

"Mr. Dunbar tells me that you have been in the community for a while," she said.

"Yes, I have. I've been at the Hook ranch for several years, and I was at another one before that."

A waiter appeared behind me and asked if we were ready to order. We all agreed to the plate lunch, which was sliced ham, scalloped potatoes, and pudding.

As the waiter left, I said to Dunbar, "I thought this was a small lunch."

"It is. We're not having the roast fowl, asparagus, pickled herring, cheesecake, and white wine."

"I understand."

Mrs. Deville spoke again in her pleasant way. "I wouldn't want to keep you in suspense, Mr. Ryerson. I'm working on a business opportunity."

"I hope it goes well for you."

"Thank you. I've been in the restaurant and café business, and I think I might like to try it again."

"I see. Well, I know something about cooking for other people, but I don't know much about the business aspect."

"Oh, I wasn't hinting at that. I even have a possible location. The place that used to be called the LaSalle."

"Oh, yes. Down at the end of the street. It's been vacant for a few years."

"So I understand. I'm seeing about getting it going again."

"That's good. Even in a small town, it's good to have more than one place to go. Gives people a choice."

"Yes, it does. And we try not to make it the same. I'm thinking of doing it in café style, like it was before."

"So you're moving along with your plans."

She smiled. "I believe I am. I have been at it for a few days, but there are several aspects to manage. I am at the point now where I am on the lookout for a bright employee."

A tenseness came into my face. "I don't know if I—"

"I can do any part of it myself," she said. "Cook, wait on customers, wash dishes, clean up. But I can't do it all. I am thinking I would like to have a girl for the kitchen and a girl for the front."

I relaxed. I was not going to have to turn down anything or make myself uncomfortable with this gracious woman. "I might know someone." I lowered my voice. "I have a niece, a very capable girl. I cannot speak for her, of course, but I could mention it to her." As I said it, I realized that Dunbar might have prepared Mrs. Deville for this possibility.

"Thank you very much. I would appreciate it. Personal recommendations can be very useful. Of course, a person might find reliable help by putting a sign in the window, but I'd rather not start that way."

"Yes," I said. "And once the townsfolk know you are opening a business, you may have people coming around to ask."

"That, too." She turned to Dunbar, as if to include him in the conversation, but she did not say anything to him.

"I'm all in favor of it," he said. "I had apple pie in here the other day, and I had it last night in the bunkhouse. I can't see any harm in having another place to try." When no one said anything, he said, "Just being facetious, of course. I know there's a great deal more to it."

Mrs. Deville gave a short smile. "I can manage the business agreements and the ordering of supplies and all that, but like I said, I can't do all the day-to-day work myself. Getting good workers is important, and I don't always know what I'm going to find." She turned her smile to me. "And so I appreciate your help."

The waiter arrived with our plates, and we did not return to that topic.

---

I LEFT Dunbar and Mrs. Deville to continue their visit. I had already decided to talk to Vivian on this trip, and now I had an additional reason. I thought I would stop at the boardinghouse first, as she did not always take her dinner at the same time, and there was a chance she might still be there.

Mrs. Williams answered the door and invited me in. I saw that she had company in the person of Thad Coulter, so I bid him good afternoon as I stood with my hat in my hand. He was sitting by the enamel-coated stove with his hands on his knees as if he was holding up his weight. His hat, coat, and stick were placed on a chair nearby.

He spoke in a loud voice. "Hello, Rye. How are you? How is everything at the ranch?"

"Normal, I suppose, with the exception of what happened to one of the hired hands, which I assume everyone has heard about."

Mrs. Williams nodded.

"Oh, yes," said Coulter, in a matter-of-fact way. "Sorry to hear about it."

I directed my attention to Mrs. Williams, who stood with her hands together in front of her apron. "I stopped to see if Vivian is here."

"She's gone back to work."

"I'll see if I can find her there. Sorry to trouble you."

"No trouble at all." Her smile seemed to have a trace of apology.

"Thank you. I'll see you later." As I nodded to each of them, I saw on the mantel clock that the time was one-thirty.

I found Vivian in the mercantile, near the entrance as I walked in. Her cheeks had their usual blush, and her expression was clear.

"Uncle Rye. I didn't expect to see you. It's only Friday."

"Um, yes. Mr. Dunbar and I made a trip with the wagon. We had to bring in the . . . well, I'm sure you heard about what was found out on the range yesterday."

Her face had gone serious, but it was not clouded up. "Kent."

"Yes. I'm sorry. I couldn't quite get the right words." I looked around. "I thought we might be able to talk for a few minutes. I stopped at the boarding-house, but Mrs. Williams said you had already gone back to work."

"I didn't know you were in town."

"I suppose it can wait. There's nothing urgent."

"Let me see if I can get away for a little while. I don't want you to have to wait until some other time if it's not necessary. I know you have your own things to do. Wait here, if you don't mind."

She walked into the center of the store, and I heard voices. A few minutes later, she reappeared, wearing a wheat-colored wool overcoat and a pair of tan gloves. "I said I would be back in less than half an hour."

"Thank you. I don't think we'll be long."

A cool breeze was blowing, and it lessened when we turned off the main street. I thought she was waiting for me to speak, so I began.

"I'm sorry for any distress or sadness you're feeling."

"Please don't worry about me," she said. "To be sure, it's unsettling, but I don't feel that it has come very close to me."

"I know that he had . . . an interest in you."

"Well, yes. But it was not anything serious. At least on my part. I know he was hoping, or wishing, that we were farther along, but I was not—how do they say?–transported."

I felt some of the tension flow out of me. "I didn't know, and there was no reason I should. But he did give me to understand, in the last conversation that he and I had by ourselves, that he had what you might call hopes. Not quite expectations, I guess, but—"

"I think I know what you mean. Maybe I'm being

too roundabout about this. So I can just say that he expressed his hopes to me. The last time I saw him. But I told him I could not go along with them at that time."

"You mean you—"

"Yes. I turned him down. I'm sure it made him sad, but I don't think it had anything to do with what happened to him. And I've told myself I can't let myself feel guilty about it."

I was surprised at her fortitude. She was not as much of a little girl as I thought. "You turned him down. Have you told anyone else about this?"

"Deputy Caryl. And in a more indirect way, Mr. Fell. He seemed anxious to console me, and I assured him there was nothing that serious between Kent and me."

"Even though Kent gave others to believe there was."

"Oh, yes. That was what Mr. Fell thought, that we were as good as engaged."

"And yet you never were."

"Oh, no. Like I said, he came to the brink of it, and I discouraged him."

"And that was on the last day that anyone saw him?"

"Yes. It was in the early evening, a short while after dark. He was waiting for me when I left work for the day."

I cast my mind back. "That would have been between the time Dunbar and I saw you in the store and the time we saw him in the saloon." I recalled an image of Kent Norland standing with his hands in the pockets of his deerskin-colored coat. "It was later in the evening when I saw you again at the boardinghouse."

"That all sounds correct."

"So let me ask you one other thing, and don't be afraid to tell me if it's too personal."

"Not at all. Go ahead."

"Did he, in the process of expressing his hopes, offer you a token or anything of that nature?"

"Oh, no. It did not go that far. Does someone think he gave me something?"

"Not that I know of. He just seemed so confident when he talked to me earlier."

Her voice was steady as she said, "I know it made him sad. And some people have said that maybe he went away because of his disappointment."

"I don't think he left. All of his belongings were still at the bunkhouse. They still are, until the deputy can find an address to send them to."

"That makes me feel better, that I did not send him away, although I did not think I did. That leaves other questions unanswered, but—"

"That's what Deputy Caryl is here for."

"I hope he finds out something. For as much as I am trying not to let myself feel guilty for any of this, I can't help feel bad about Kent."

We came to the end of a block. "This might be as far as we have to go," I said. "We could turn around and go back."

"I have plenty of time. We haven't been gone that long."

The breeze felt stronger when we turned around. After a minute, I remembered the other topic I wanted to mention.

"You remember Mr. Dunbar," I said.

"Of course."

"Well, he has a friend, a woman named Mrs. Deville, who is staying in town."

"I've heard of her. A young widow, staying at the hotel."

"I didn't know she was a widow, but it goes with her general presence. At any rate, she has told me that she is working on a plan to reopen the LaSalle Café."

"I've heard something of that as well."

"It shouldn't be that much of a secret. She said she has been making arrangements, and she told me she was on the lookout for a bright employee. I told her I knew of a capable young woman and I would mention it to you."

"Well, thank you. That sounds like a good possibility."

"I think she might want someone to work in the front part, waiting on customers and taking orders, as well as someone to work in the kitchen, wash dishes, do the cleaning, and so forth."

"The front part sounds like something I could try, but I wouldn't want to think I'm above any of it."

"That is along the lines of what I thought. If you'd like, I can tell her you might be interested, but I know you can speak for yourself well enough."

"Thank you. I can, but I don't know how soon I could go to see her. It gets dark early. And I don't want to lose out on the chance by waiting for tomorrow. So if you don't mind telling her—"

"Not at all. You never know what will come of it, but it might help you get out of a place as we've talked about."

"That would be good."

I walked her the rest of the way to the store and agreed to see her later. I counted myself lucky at not having to talk to Fell, and I set out to look for Mrs. Deville.

As I walked, my thoughts went back to an earlier part of the conversation with Vivian. I believed I had answered my question about how many people knew about the pendant with the diamond and the emerald. George Marven and I knew where it came from, and someone else knew where it was now.

---

THE OLD PALE-GREEN lettering of the LaSalle Café was beginning to chip and flake on the inside of the glass, and the outside had not been cleaned since summer rain blew from the south, which did not happen often. I stood close to the window to cut off the glare from the afternoon daylight, and I saw Mrs. Deville inside, talking to Dunbar. I felt as if I was in a theatre, watching a silent performance between a cowboy and a lady who needed to have her dining room painted. I tapped on the window, and they both turned. Mrs. Deville beckoned for me to come in.

The bell on the door tinkled as I walked inside.

"You found me," said Mrs. Deville.

"I asked at the hotel, and they said you were out, so this was my next guess."

"Mr. Dunbar was good enough to come with me. I don't know the town well enough yet to go wandering around by myself."

"It's just as well." I stopped short of saying anything more, although I had my thoughts, given the errand that Dunbar and I had been on earlier in the day.

"There's a great deal of dust here," she said. "My

good fortune is that the last owners left a broom, a mop, and a small pile of rags."

"I thought I heard they left an inventory of plates and cups and utensils."

"They did. It all needs to be cleaned." She frowned. "But it's not anything that can't be dealt with. If I can get some coal in here tomorrow, and heat some water, this place will warm up as well."

"I would think so. Location is in your favor. The coal and drayage company is across the street. By the way, I had a chance to talk to my niece, and she says she is interested in the prospect."

"Oh, good. Thank you. That would be for the work out front here, I assume. I won't look for anyone else for that part until I've talked to her, then. I don't expect to have work for her right away, anyway. A few days, at least."

"I can let her know. She's working now, as you may know. At the store. She might be able to see you in the middle of the day tomorrow, when she goes to dinner."

"That should be all right. I expect to be here."

I glanced around at the dining area. In spite of the cobwebs and the dust, it did not look bad.

The doorbell jingled, and the door opened partway. A person in drab clothes was obscured by the frame of the door itself as a woman's voice carried through the opening.

"Can I come in?"

"Yes," said Mrs. Deville. "Come on in."

The door opened farther, and the person stepped in. She was dressed in a hooded overcoat of coarse grey and black wool, but I recognized her by her almost muddy complexion and green eyes. She pushed back the hood, and her dark brown hair remained tucked inside the coat. She stood by herself, and as my gaze shifted, I saw Sophie peering in through the glass pane of the door.

"Let the little girl come in," said "Mrs. Deville. "She doesn't have to stand outside alone."

"I don't want her to be any trouble. I came to talk to you about work."

"It's no trouble. Bring her in, and we can talk."

The woman turned around and spoke to the girl, and Sophie walked in. She looked around, and her eyes lit on Dunbar.

"I know you."

"Hush," said the woman. She directed her attention to Mrs. Deville. "I heard that you are opening this business again." Her words were clear and deliberate.

"I am," said Mrs. Deville.

"I would like to ask if you are hiring anyone." Again, her language sounded careful and prepared.

"I am considering it. I have one person in mind already for the work of waiting on customers. The other situation is mostly in the kitchen—helping prepare food, washing dishes, and cleaning up when we close at night. When I say prepare food, I mean peeling potatoes, cutting up carrots and onions, and things like that. At least to begin with."

"I can do that. I wouldn't know how to do big meals."

"How about washing dishes, scrubbing pots, and cleaning the floor?"

"I'm not afraid of any of that." The woman hesitated and then spoke in the deliberate way she had used earlier. "I want to find honest work, ma'am. I want a way of supporting myself and this little girl, and I don't want to have to resort to a low way of making a living. I'll do my best for you and stay out of the way."

Mrs. Deville regarded the woman and the girl and came back to the woman. "What is your name?"

"Madeline, ma'am. Madeline Osborn."

"I believe you when you say you can do the work. There's quite a bit of work to be done before I can open up. You can see for yourself. Regular cleaning. Can you start tomorrow?"

"Yes, I can. What time?"

"Let's say nine o'clock. I'll be sure to have things ready by then."

"I'll be here. Thank you very much." The woman nodded to Dunbar and to me, took Sophie by the hand, and walked out with the doorbell jingling.

Mrs. Deville took a long breath. "I hope I don't regret hiring the first person that comes along, but I was taken by what she said about wanting to make an honest living. I suppose I could have waited and asked about her." She spoke to Dunbar. "Do you know them?"

"Rye and I met them on the street the other day. The little girl was admiring one of the wagon horses."

She turned to me. "Do you know them?"

"I know of them. I know the woman's first name. I believe she's done various work around town. And I believe she has some sense of responsibility, taking in the little girl as she has done. I don't know where the child comes from, and I don't know where this woman Madeline lived before she came here."

"Everyone has a past," said Mrs. Deville. "Some better than others. And people have a right to try to work their way up. She's got that little girl to take care of, and she wants to work—says she's not afraid of it. I don't suppose I should be, either."

"I agree," said Dunbar. "As I told Rye the other day, there's not all that much that separates us from the less fortunate—some, but it's not as if we live in different worlds. I would rather break bread with these people than with the wealthy or the cruel."

The lady of the premises smiled. "In a business like this, we often eat in the kitchen with the help."

---

HAVING AGREED to meet Dunbar in the saloon as before, in the early evening, I went about my errands. I timed my visit to the mercantile so I would finish at about the time Vivian finished work for the day.

The center aisle was empty, and I saw no one around, so I walked to the counter. I stared at the brown-shouldered hawk on the shelf above until I heard footsteps. Raymond Fell came out of the back room, straightening his cuffs.

"Hallo," he said. "I didn't know if we'd get anyone else before we closed. I've got the kids making price tags. I'll get 'em out here. I suppose you have an order." He looked at me not quite straight on, as if with special attention, and his nose came into profile.

"Yes," I said. I handed him the small sheet of paper.

"Oh, it's a short one today. This won't take long."

He went in back, and a minute later, he came out following the two young people. Alan went one way, and Vivian went the other. Fell stood in place behind the counter and brushed at his sleeve.

He turned his eyes to me and said, "I was very

sorry to hear of what happened to your young ranch hand."

"Very sad. We hope the deputy finds out something."

"Oh, yes. I'm glad everyone else is all right. Including yourself."

"Thank you."

"And as always, I appreciate your business."

I did not have an answer. Silence hung in the air. Fell's hand moved toward his watch, then stopped. He had a frozen half-smile, and his eyes seemed to gaze at the middle distance.

Alan set a ten-pound bag of flour on the counter. With his head bent forward, he said, "You have dried apples on the list, but it doesn't say how much."

"Three or four pounds," I said. "Make it four."

"Make sure they go in a cloth sack," said the boss.

Vivian set four cans of peaches on the other end of the counter. "I didn't know you were still in town."

"I'm to meet Dunbar a little later on," I said. "We won't stay out late. Then we'll go home. If you'd like, I'll see you home now, as it's dark. I've got the wagon here."

"That would be convenient. It won't be long till I'm done."

"I'll wait outside once I have my order."

Fell's eyes followed her as she walked away. He came back to me. "Not bad weather we've been having, for as late in the year as it is."

"It can turn bad any time, you know."

"Oh, yes. But I hope it's fair for you tonight. Moon's at about half, so the visibility is good."

Alan set a lumpy flour sack on the counter. "Here's the apples."

"Don't go away," said the boss. "You can help him carry these things out."

Vivian set a small burlap sack of coffee beans on her end of the counter without speaking and moved away. The storekeeper flicked a glance and came back to the bill he was filling out.

"Very well," he said. "Sign here, and the boy will help you out." As I signed, he said, "Thanks again for your business."

I carried the coffee and the dried apples, and Alan carried the rest. At the wagon, I thanked him. Remembering what it was like at his age, I asked him if he was glad to be getting off work.

"I suppose," he said. "After we close up, I have to put out mousetraps. Then I have to pick 'em all up in the morning and throw out the dead mice."

"But you'll be done pretty soon this evening."

"At the store. Then I stop at Mrs. Fife's and put up her chickens for the night. I close 'em up at night and let 'em out in the morning."

"Chickens."

"She calls them her pretty chickens. I don't see them as all that pretty, but someone has to look out for them."

"It's good of you to help. And think of all the people who are glad to have the eggs."

"If those hens all turned into fried chicken, it would be all right with me. But as long as they're alive, we don't want the raccoons and weasels to get to them."

# 7

I STOPPED THE WAGON IN FRONT OF THE boardinghouse and climbed down to walk Vivian to the door. I had told her of my conversation with Mrs. Deville, and I did not feel anything pressing for my time.

"If you're not in a hurry, you could come in for a few minutes," she said.

"I suppose I could." I had a favorable impression of her landlady, Mrs. Williams, and I welcomed the opportunity to see her when Thad Coulter had taken his busy body elsewhere. I followed Vivian up the steps.

As I understood it, Mrs. Williams had a capacity for four lodgers in her house, but because she preferred not to have men and women under the same roof, she had only two tenants at present—Vivian and a woman who cleaned offices and businesses and came in at about ten.

Vivian let herself in with her key, and I followed.

Mrs. Williams came into the front room as I took off my hat.

"Oh, Mr. Ryerson," she said. "How good it is to see you. I was hoping you did not feel shunted away when you were here earlier."

"Not at all. I was on my way to find Vivian, which I did. I was there again, picking up supplies, when she finished her work for the day, so I offered to see her home."

"And so well that you did. A person shouldn't have to worry about walking home in the dark, but with what has happened, we can't be so sure of how safe it is in our own town. May I take your hat?"

"I don't mean to stay but for a few minutes."

"Oh, no. You have to stay for supper. It's almost ready. You can't be in that much of a hurry."

I allowed myself to look at her as I smiled. She had a pleasant appearance, being a few years younger than I was and in good condition—not stout and not lean, grey-haired but not wrinkled. She had hazel eyes and a clear complexion, with a faint touch of pink.

"I'm sure I have time," I said.

"Then let me take your hat."

I felt as if she had touched a soft spot, and yet I had not been one to put up a barricade against women. I had just not ever met what seemed to be the right one, and I had met several who I was sure were not. I gave her my hat, and she offered me the upholstered armchair I had sat in when I had the confidential conversation with Vivian the week before.

Mrs. Williams went into the kitchen, and Vivian said she was going to her room to leave her coat and gloves. She returned in a minute, with a cheerful air about her.

"Let me set the table for another person." She moved to the dining area, which was separated by a wide arch from the sitting room. She spoke a couple of words to Mrs. Williams, who was farther in, in the kitchen.

Supper consisted of beef stew, which Mrs. Williams served from a large bowl into smaller ones at the end of the table, and bread, which came out covered with a cloth from a bread box on the side-board. I knew she baked her own bread, so I was pleased to try it.

I found myself sitting across from Vivian. Mrs. Williams sat next to her, closer to the kitchen. The atmosphere seemed light and sociable, in contrast with the bunkhouse, where as a general practice, men ate first and then talked.

"And how are things out in the country?" asked Mrs. Williams.

I knew that her late husband had worked for a feed and grain company and that she was conversant in farm and ranch matters. I said, "About normal for this time of year. We've shipped the steers for the fall, and the cattle are turned out to winter pasture. The hands are still around because the boss wants to build a shed to store feed."

"That's good, to be building."

"It is, and I'm glad he doesn't do it the way some outfits do, build a little shed now and then, and have a dozen mismatched things with cattle and sheep wandering among them."

After a short silence, she said, "We were sorry to hear of the incident. It's always sad when a young person goes, and yet there are so many ways for it to happen."

"Yes, and he has a family somewhere."

"It must be very difficult for them when they learn of it."

I had understood that she had not had children herself and that she enjoyed having young people under her roof, unlike the old biddy type of woman who sometimes ran a boardinghouse. "Yes, and as you suggest, it happens all too often. Young people come out here for adventure, and to make a living, and there are so many dangers in the work, in the weather, and in . . . other unforeseen things."

The table went quiet for a moment.

"On the brighter side," said Vivian, "there's a lady in town who is opening up the LaSalle Café again. I am planning to talk to her about work."

"Oh."

"Uncle Rye knows her."

I said, "She's a friend of this man named Dunbar. He's new at the ranch. Seems like a good hand, and educated in some way. The lady is well-mannered as well. She says she's been in the business before and is not afraid of the work." I realized I had mixed my quotations, but I left it at that.

"There will be plenty of that," said Mrs. Williams. "Work. But if she's done it before, she knows what she's getting into. Running a business in a small town is not easy. People are so jealous. And nosy."

I recalled her visitor at midday, and I wondered how long it would be until he found his way to the new business.

My silence may have weighed upon her, for she changed the subject. "I'm sure you have ways of passing the time when your workers leave for the winter and the days grow long indoors."

"I get by. We burn wood, you know, so that gives me plenty to do during the daylight. Gather and cut firewood. And I have other things as well." Thinking of something that might interest her, I said, "For example, I ventured to sew a quilt—not one of your patchwork quilts, but a camp quilt. I sewed a wool blanket between two sheets of lightweight canvas. I tacked it in several places in the middle as well. Just stitching it all around the edges took me quite a bit of time. The better part of a few days."

"Oh, yes."

"I had a bit of trouble with the cloths bunching up and coming out uneven. I learned which directions to push in the pins to hold the fabric together and which direction to sew the stitch. Even then, I had to cut away some of the unevenness. But the end product looked all right, and it works well for keeping you warm."

Mrs. Williams laughed. "Cooks and seamstresses learn how to make their mistakes unnoticeable."

I said, "As a cook, I've had to make some of my mistakes unnoticeable by throwing them out. I won't call myself a seamstress or anything of the sort, so I can't say much about that."

"If you've sewn a quilt, you've done something."

"Yes, and it's practical."

---

THE MANTEL CLOCK showed a little after seven when I left the boardinghouse and went to meet up with Dunbar. I found him in the Double Eagle Saloon, where a few patrons had already gathered. Tobacco smoke formed a haze under the brass lamps overhead, and the golden eagle sat on its perch above the two pillars. Dunbar seemed to be listening to a song from the piano, but he turned and gave me his attention.

"How goes it?"

"Well enough. I told Vivian that Mrs. Deville was looking forward to seeing her, I picked up a few things at the store, and I gave in to an invitation to have supper at the boardinghouse."

"It sounds like you did well."

"I think so. Have you eaten?"

"A morsel of cheese and a crust of bread. Fit for the journey home."

I wondered if the whiskey glass on the bar had made him poetic or if the music had put him in the spirit.

"I might allow myself to have a beer while you finish your drink."

"I'm in no hurry. It's my first one, and I've barely touched it. I've just been biding my time, keeping my eyes and ears open."

I had the impression, as I had had before, that he had taken an interest in the Kent Norland case to a greater degree than some of the townspeople, although they all seemed interested in its conversational value.

My order came, and I took a sip. "I wonder how the deputy is faring."

"He's still in town. We saw him again in the dining room."

A loud voice down the bar caused us both to turn. The round-shouldered lout in the bowler hat, from the week before, was calling for whiskey.

"Do you know who that is?" asked Dunbar.

"No, I don't."

The man paid for his whiskey, drank it up, and left.

We were standing closer to the piano than on our previous visit, and so the music was loud and clear when a man sat down and began to play. I had seen him at one of the roundup camps, and he was standing with other men I recognized. Now seated, he banged on the keys and chanted a song about a cowpuncher who lost all his money in a parlor house and lost his horse and saddle at the gambling table. After one song, the man went to join his friends, who had been jeering at him.

A couple of minutes later, another man stepped up to stand by the piano. He was wearing a sheepskin coat and a black hat with a ridged crown. He was above average height, lean, with a pale face and deep-set eyes. His hat was tipped to one side, and he spoke in a smooth Southern voice.

"Good evenin', ladies and gentlemen, though I don't see any ladies here yet. This is a sing-for-your-supper night, for me. I'm passin' through, tryin' to get back to my great home state of Texas after some time in Montana. Let me sing a tune for you, which I wrote myself. I don't play the piano, so I'll just sing it, and if you like, you can put something in my hat when it goes around. My name's Deke McGinley. The song is called 'Rustlers' Doom,' and it goes like this."

He pulled in a breath, squared his shoulders in a theatrical pose, held his hands out palm down, and delivered his song.

ON A BLEAK WYOMING plain
In a cold late April rain
A pair of fugitive rustlers
Pushed their horses through the gloom.

One of them was burning hot
In the lung where he'd been shot,
And he knew the time was coming
When he'd have to face his doom.

His companion urged him on,
Said they'd hole up till the dawn,
Then push forward to the mountains,
Where they'd find a hideaway.

But the wounded one had doubt,
For his strength was playing out,
And his eyelids now grew heavy
And the world was turning grey.

So he called his comrade near,
Said, "You'll have to leave me here,"
And he tumbled from the saddle,
Knowing soon the end would come.

"Do me one last favor, Ed,
For I know I'll soon be dead,
Let me have my saddle blanket
So at least I will be warm."

As the day was sinking low
And the raindrops turned to snow,
Partner Ed sat still and pondered
What would be the best for him—

He considered what he'd need,
And in line with the outlaw creed,
Said, "I don't think you will need it
Quite as much as I will, Jim."

So he left his partner there
In the damp and chilling air
As he rode off in the twilight
With a saddled horse in tow,

And the storm clouds settled in
Where the light had grown more dim
For the man who now lay huddled
In the silent falling snow.

Then came seven days of death
In the blizzard's killing breath
As the snow packed deep and frozen
On the contours of the land,

Till the weather drifted south,
And the ranch hands ventured out
As they searched for strays and stragglers
That might wear their outfit's brand.

'Neath the blanket of the storm
First they found a human form
In the lee of knee-high sagebrush
Where he'd curled up tight to die.

In a gully farther west
Next they found the final rest
Of a horse that wore a bridle
And the saddle lay nearby.

As they climbed up on a hill
Came the cry of ravens shrill
From half a mile on upward
Where the pines began to grow.

There they found a second horse
Stretched out dead just like the first
Bare upon a frozen pedestal
Of hard, wind-sculpted snow.

Now the ravens' piercing cry
Led them farther up on high
Where a boulder offered shelter
To a man who sat below.

But he did not move or stir
In his coat that looked like fur—
'Twas a pair of saddle blankets
And an inch of drifted snow.

A round of applause sounded, and the man's hat went around. Dunbar and I each put in a quarter and passed it on.

"That's quite a song," I said to Dunbar.

"Yes. It would be nice if justice was always that neat."

"I noticed that it starts out on a Wyoming plain. I imagine he changes it to Montana or Nebraska, depending on where he goes."

"If he's on his way home, Nebraska could be on the trail."

Someone called out for another song.

The man named Deke gave a crooked smile and said, "I would, but I don't know any. I'm workin' on another one, though."

"He seems pretty independent," I said. "He doesn't sing other people's songs, and he doesn't use an instrument. He had to work a long time on this one. What do you think he does for a living?"

Dunbar kept his voice low. "He reminds me of someone who just got out of prison. He may have traded up for that coat. I try not to judge people, though."

I had occasion to think once again that Dunbar, younger though he was, might have seen parts of life and formed insights that I never would. I said, "He's making his way, anyway."

"Oh, yes. And he knows his verse and meter better than some of the troubadours I've heard."

A touch on my shoulder caused me to turn. I drew back at seeing a face I had last seen outside the mercantile. A small jolt of alarm ran through me.

"What is it, Alan?"

His hair was tousled, as he had taken off his cap, and his face was flushed from coming in from the cold air. "Excuse me, Mr. Ryerson. I'm sorry for bothering you in here, but there's someone who would like to talk to you and this other gentleman, the man in the black hat."

"Mr. Dunbar."

"She didn't say his name, but I assumed she meant him."

*She.* I drew my brows together. "Who is it?"

"I don't like to say someone's name in a place like this, sir. But she's the one who's going to go to work for the lady that's starting up the LaSalle Café."

"The woman who takes care of the little girl."

"That's the one. She says she would like to talk to the two of you if it's not too much trouble."

"I don't think it is." I turned to Dunbar. "Did you follow that?"

"Yes, I did. I think we can find time."

I turned to the boy again. "We'll be out in a couple of minutes. We just have to finish our drinks."

"I'll tell her, and I'll wait out front."

Alan was standing at the edge of the light when we went outside. He was wearing a knit cap now, and he had his shoulders hunched with his hands in his coat pockets. We walked up close to him so we would not have to speak out loud.

"Where is she?" I asked.

"In the alley on the other side of the street."

With his hands still in his pockets, he made a rigid turn and began walking west past the clothing store. At the corner, he shifted to his left and crossed the street, where the windows of the bank reflected the moonlight. He led us along the shadowed side of the bank, across the street from the livery stable, where light showed around the edges of the door.

At the alley, he turned left. The ground crunched under our feet as we walked behind the bank, the grain broker's office, the small mercer and milliner's shop, and the post office. He stopped in the shadows behind a vacant business. One human form became visible, and then a second. Our party of three waited for them to come forward.

"Who's here?" said Dunbar in a low voice to Alan.

"A fellow who thinks he has to look after her."

The woman in the hooded coat stepped forward, and a man followed at her elbow. He wore a short-billed cap and a long coat not much heavier than a duster.

The woman said, "You need to go, Critter. I need to talk to them, that's all."

The man muttered something.

"No. You need to leave. This is confidential, and no one else needs to hear it. Just go."

"I'll go now, too," said Alan. Gravel crunched, and he walked away in the direction of the bank.

"Thanks," I said. I did not have time to give him a tip, and I was not sure whether he would have wanted it.

The woman's voice sounded again. "Go, Critter."

The man was slender and of middle height. I did not think I had seen him before. He was being obstinate, and I believed he thought we were going to be clients of hers.

"Look," said Dunbar. "If the woman says she doesn't want you around, you need to leave. She says she wants to talk to us. If you think something else is up, you're wrong."

"Just leave," she said.

I could feel his sullenness in the dark as he stood in place and moved his head side to side.

In a mushy voice, he said, "I don't like it." Pushing

himself to his toes from his flat-footed stance, he leaned to the right and spit. With his hands in his coat pockets, he leaned forward and stalked away, following Alan.

Dunbar spoke to the woman. "I don't know if you think this is a good place to talk."

"He might come back. He thinks he wants to own me."

"Where would you like to go?"

"How about in the back of the café? I don't think there's anyone there right now."

"I don't think there is," said Dunbar.

We walked together down the alley to the east, toward the moon on the rise. We came to a cross street and a second one. We turned and followed it across the main street, with the mercantile a few doors down on our left, all in the dark now. Past the main street, we turned right into the next alley. We walked more than half a block and came to a stop behind the café. No lights showed, but the moonlight was better on this side of the building in the early part of the evening.

"I hope this is all right," said Dunbar.

"I think so."

We waited, and she began in her deliberate way.

"I have something to say that I think more than one person should know. I have kind of an intuition that you might be some kind of an investigator, so . . . "

Dunbar surprised me by saying, "For the sake of conversation, I won't say I'm not."

"And you're a friend of this lady. She seems like someone you can trust."

"I'm quite sure you're right."

"I appreciate it that she's giving me a chance to

make an honest living. My life has had a lot of low spots, and it's not easy."

"I understand."

"Maybe you do. You don't have to know all the facts to have a general idea. And I'm sure you've seen some things."

"Some."

Her hooded head was downcast as she said, "And I have a kind of intuition that I'm not going to live long."

"I would encourage you not to think that way."

"It's just something I feel. And it's part of why I thought I should tell someone something."

"I think I can say I understand that, too."

She raised her head and sniffled. She looked at each of us in turn and said, "You are both grown men, you act civil, and I imagine you both know something about the world and aren't afraid of the truth, even if it's kind of blunt."

I felt that she was getting back into that mode of speech in which she had thought out what she was going to say. I shook my head. "Don't worry about me."

Dunbar said, "Or me. Go ahead."

"Well, as you might have guessed, I've resorted to making my living from men. It's not the only thing I've done, but it's something I've gone back to, and once they know you, it's hard to get out of. So that's one main way I've made a living in this town up until now."

I nodded, as if to say that this truth was not too strong for me. At the same time, I hoped she did not go too far, although I did not know how far that was.

She went on. "And one of my customers was this young man who just died."

I felt a tightening in my stomach.

"I was never more than second-best, if that, but I was always good enough when he had what he called his needs. He was all over me, and then he would say he felt guilty, because he had his eye on a good girl, and he didn't know if he would ever be good enough for her."

I felt a sickness as I recalled how dedicated he made himself out to be when he showed me the emerald and diamond. My thoughts went on to the last time I saw him, which would have been after Vivian turned him down, and it occurred to me that he might have disappeared in this person's direction.

I said, "If you don't mind my asking, do you remember when the last time was that you saw him?"

Her eyes were calm in the faint light. "Yes, I do. It was the last night anyone saw him."

"Saw him alive," said Dunbar. "It *is* thought that someone transported him to the place where he was found. But I don't mean to take you off the topic."

"I don't know what else I have to say. I just felt that I needed to tell someone that much, in case it ever mattered."

"It might, and we appreciate it," said Dunbar. "And I assure you we know how to keep things to ourselves."

"I thought you did." She sniffed.

"And before we part company, I wonder if I might ask a question."

"What is it?"

"Do you know of anyone who might have had a

strong enough reason to lift a hand against this young man?"

"Not really," she said. "Not a strong reason. This fellow he worked with, named Ned, was jealous of him because of the girl he was courting, but I don't think it was that strong."

I let the tightness pass through me.

"Anything else? Did he ever mention anyone?"

Her voice remained steady. "He said Cage Whitman had a grudge against him from the time when they knew each other in Fetterman. He said he wasn't there for very long."

"Who is Cage Whitman?" Dunbar moved his eyes from her to me as he asked the question.

I did not know, so I let her answer.

"He's the doorman at the Blue Diamond. But I don't think it was anything serious. Cage is sarcastic to everyone."

"I see. Can you think of anything else?"

"Not at the moment."

"How about . . . Critter?"

"Oh, no. He's just gotten stuck on me in the last little while. He hasn't been in town for very long."

"I suppose that's good enough, then. If you'd like, we can walk you back to where we met you. Or if you prefer, we can go separate ways."

"I'd just as soon have someone go along. I don't live far from there."

We went back the way we came, and no one spoke the whole way. I was glad not to find anyone waiting behind the vacant business next to the post office. When we stopped, she said, "Thanks" and walked away in the shadows between two houses on the other side of the alley.

At the corner once again, in front of the bank, Dunbar and I paused. No one was in view up and down the street.

Dunbar said, "I thought she might know something else. Well, I'm sure she knows plenty of other things, but maybe this was all that she thought was pertinent. Still, you never know if some bit of information might be useful."

"Even if it is disagreeable." It was bad enough that Norland would go from Vivian to couple with a woman of the streets, but what stuck in my craw at least as bad was that he mentioned the good girl when he was feeling sorry for himself with the woman.

"I can see why you would feel that way, and you may not need my advice, but I think it's better to think of it as just information at this point. By the way, do you know this Cage Whitman?"

"Not at all. It's the first time I've heard the name."

"What's the Blue Diamond?"

"You take me for a man of the world. It's a road ranch on the main trail northeast of here. About five miles."

I could see Dunbar placing it in his mind. It was in the opposite direction from the Hook ranch, and the wagon was waiting.

"Then we won't go there tonight," he said.

# 8

Ned Hacker was smoking a cigarette after breakfast, and the others were drinking coffee.

The boss said, "I think I'll go to town today to order materials for this building. Ned, you can go with me to drive the wagon."

Ned looked at the cigarette in his hand. "Why didn't we go yesterday?" His rough voice sounded quarrelsome even when he was not.

The boss was used to him. In a matter-of-fact tone, he said, "I was still working on my lists and figuring how much we would need. And you might not have gotten to go if I had gone yesterday."

Dunbar and Tyler went about their work, and I was left with a free hour in the late morning. The weather being dry and not very cold, though not sunny, I decided to go out and gather a wheelbarrow load of sagebrush branches. The wood was not good for a large, roaring fire, but I knew it burned well and gave off a bit of an aroma.

My work took me down into a draw not far from where I had seen the goose go through the fence. I had a mattock, which was good for grubbing out dead branches. As I picked them up, I wondered if they were similar to the furze faggots that Dunbar had spoken of.

My thought came back to the present as a dead smell entered my nostrils. Searching around, I saw that it came from a hole in the ground where Tyler and I had buried a pony about six months earlier. The pony was named Pedro, pronounced with a long *e* by the ranch hands, and it had come with the ranch when Wes Galvin bought the place. The previous owner, Hook, had bought it for his son, but the little boy had died from a rattlesnake bite, and the parents were never able to overcome their disappointment. When they sold the ranch, they left the pony with the other livestock. It wandered in the horse pasture until it died.

Now I saw where coyotes, or perhaps badgers, had dug down into the pony's resting place. With my mattock, I dragged a great deal of the dirt back into the hole, but some of it was stuck in the grass and the sagebrush. The smell began to fade, but I did not think the grave was repaired enough. What dirt I had put in was loose, and the animals would not have to work hard to dig again.

Looking around at the hillside, I hit upon the idea of covering the area with clumps of yucca, or soapweed, as the punchers called it. There was quite of it growing on the slopes of the draw. The narrow leaves were sharp as needles. After a few swings with the mattock, I improved my aim so that the tips did not jab through my gloves. In about half an hour, I had twenty-five to thirty plants packed together in an area of about ten feet square.

I took off my hat, said a couple of words, and went back to picking up sagebrush.

I told Tyler about the incident when we went out to work with the horses after noon dinner.

"Grave robbers," he said. "But that's scavengers for you."

We went on to the lesson for the day.

"What do you know about tying up a horse?" he asked.

I thought of where to start. "Well, you want to tie him high enough and short enough so that he can't step over the rope and get tangled. That goes for whether you're in camp or here in the yard. Like you said the other day, a horse's reaction is to pull back. If you tie him too loose or too low and he gets wrapped up, he's hard to get loose. Even if you tie them up right, some horses pull back just to be doing it. Some pull back and upwards and shake a little. Others pull straight back, set on their haunches, and see if they can break a rope or halter. Some aren't satisfied until they pull a hitching rail apart."

"That's good."

"And look out for rope burns if you grab a loose rope."

"That, too."

"What I don't know is how to break a horse from pulling back."

"Neither do I. I thought I did, but I don't. One thing I have done is not tie the horse. Leave the rope loose. Then when he pulls back, he doesn't have anything to pull against. Ruins his game."

"Partner ties up just fine."

"Sure he does. But this other horse I'm going to work with today is a buster."

We saddled our horses and went for a ride. It was uneventful, which I believe was our objective. Tyler was not a great talker out on the trail, and I rode behind him a good part of the time, watching him sway with the motion of the horse.

I was left to my own thoughts, and they drifted back to the conversation that Dunbar and I had with Madeline Osborn. She said she could not think of anyone who had a strong enough reason to stifle Kent Norland. In my suspicions, I kept coming back to Raymond Fell. But jealousy over a girl did not seem that compelling, even if his jealousy was stronger than Ned Hacker's. Fell might not have known yet that Vivian had turned down the young man. He would have seen Norland waiting for her, and that could have set him off. On the other hand, he might well have sensed that Norland was not carrying the day. He had shown condescension to Norland in the saloon, and he had appeared to have plenty of self-control. And then there was the matter of Norland's personal property. I could not see why a man like Fell would have a motive to filch it. Still, Fell loomed as such an obvious possibility to me that I could not ignore it, even as I realized that I might be making it too obvious.

---

I BURNED the sagebrush in the late afternoon when the temperature was beginning to drop in the bunkhouse. I continued the fire with cedar, as I had some lengths of branches about an inch and a half thick. The fire crackled, and wisps of black smoke rose, followed by a puffy, powdery, grey smoke. The pungent smell was pleasant. I fanned the fire, and the flames burned clearer. I put on some common pieces of elm so that the fire would not burn out before the men came in.

Dunbar brought me some deer meat from the carcass hanging in the barn, as I had asked him to do. He had cut out a slab from a hindquarter, about five pounds, and it was clean as well as cold to the touch. He left it on my cutting board and went back to the barn.

A few minutes later, I heard the sound of the wagon coming to a stop. I went to the door to see if I needed to bring in anything, and I looked out in the fading light. Ned Hacker and the boss had climbed down and were looking into the bed of the wagon. To my surprise, I thought I saw Dunbar standing next to them, with his back to me. And yet he had just gone to the barn.

The puzzle ended when the man turned around. He was thinner than Dunbar, and he had no mustache. His sheepskin coat had made him look huskier. He wore a black hat that I had seen before, and I recognized his uneven smile.

"This is Deke," said the boss. "He needed work, and I thought we could use the help."

When a new man arrived at the ranch, there was often a saddle in the wagon, but all this man had was a small pasteboard valise.

"Rider?" I asked.

"Sometimes," he said in his smooth voice.

The boss spoke. "I thought we could use another hand with the building, but if he needs to ride, he can use one of the extra saddles. And there's Kent's saddle as well. Tyler can show him when the time comes."

The new arrival did not speak much during the meal or afterwards. I saw that he did not have a bedroll, so I told him he could use the blankets that were on the empty bunk. I did not tell him they were Kent Norland's, and I did not think it mattered. He looked tired. I thought he might not have eaten in a while and the food was catching up with him. He turned in early and went to sleep right away.

---

THE QUIET TROUBADOUR was clear-eyed in the morning as he ate flapjacks and drank coffee. He did not say anything about being a performer, and neither Dunbar nor I mentioned having seen him in town.

The sky had cleared overnight, and a hard frost lay on the ground. The day being Sunday, the boss said that the work on the new building would begin the next day. Other than tending to the daily chores, the men could do as they wished, but he hoped they stayed at the ranch. Through the morning, the men heated water, shaved, and took turns taking a bath behind the blanket at the far end of the bunkhouse.

After noon dinner, I told the boys I needed the table to sort beans. I told them I was not running them out, as anyone who wanted to help sort was welcome. Dunbar said he had been looking forward to it. Ned Hacker said he thought he would go to the barn, and Tyler said he thought he would, too. They invited the new hand to go along.

He smiled and said, in his cordial tone, "What do you-all do? I hope it's not too sinful." His voice had a touch of the Southern preacher.

"Oh, no," said Tyler. "We just play cards. There's a

little kerosene stove that keeps us warm. We play a three-handed game of pinochle. You can take Kent's place."

"Wal, I wouldn't want to go down there to be euchred. I don't have any money to lose, anyway."

Tyler waved his hand. "Don't worry about that. We just play for fun."

"I guess I will, then."

Dunbar set the twenty-five-pound sack of beans on the table and untied the twine. "They sewed this one good and tight," he said. "Sometimes they have the stitches three fingers apart." He set the twine aside and poured the beans into an oblong mound.

I gave him a small pan that had lost its handle. "You can put the bad ones, the rocks, and the clods in here."

Wes Galvin was reading the newspaper by the stove. He lowered the paper and said, "If there's one thing I can't stand, it's bitin' down on one of those little rocks."

"We'll get 'em," said Dunbar.

Time passed in the calm of the bunkhouse. I could hear myself breathing. From Dunbar's end, I heard the sound of beans being scooted across the tabletop, the soft rattle of another handful being dragged off the mound, and the occasional ping of a tiny rock being tossed into the pan. The boss folded his newspaper and dozed in his chair.

At long last, the butte of beans had been moved, a few at a time, and the clean beans were all back in the bag.

"These are good for now," I said. "I always rinse a batch before cooking them, and then I soak them overnight."

"Sometimes a little rock still sneaks through. It's hard to see how it can happen, but it does."

The boss was sitting by the stove and was cleaning a pair of boots with saddle soap. He said, "A bad bean at least gets cooked, and a clod melts. But the idea of biting down on a little rock gives me the shivers."

The afternoon light was beginning to fade, so I lit a lamp and hung it over the table. I was planning to make biscuits later on, so I began to mix the dry ingredients in a mixing pan.

Dunbar went to his bunk and came back with a sharpening stone in a wooden case plus a small can of oil. He took out his pocketknife and took to sharpening it in small, circular motions.

The boss said, "If you two were a little better, you could make music together."

"I hadn't thought of that," said Dunbar. "But I think I'm done." He ran his thumb across the blade and put the cover on the wooden case. As I gave my mixing spoon a few more turns, he took a short pencil out of his shirt pocket and sharpened it, shaving the wood in thin curls. He brushed the shavings into the palm of his hand, stood up, and tossed them into the stove. As he was taking his seat again, a lonesome, hooting sound carried on the air outside.

"Yon moping owl," he said.

I crossed the room and opened the door to hear the sound better. When it came, I located the owl in the leafless branches of an elm tree. As if he had seen me, the bird quit his calling and flapped away.

"He's gone now," I said. "I'm afraid I scared him off."

"Just as well," said the boss. "Some people think they bring bad luck."

Dunbar said, "The poet calls it a merry note. 'Tu-whit, tu-who: a merry note, while greasy Joan doth keel the pot.' "

I closed the door. "Greasy Joan. I guess that's me. I've got salt pork planned for us this evening. And I've got bacon rind set aside for the next pot of beans."

"This is the time of year for it," said Dunbar. "Fat-hungry people in the North would relish it. On the other hand, there's a time and place for eating oranges and pineapple."

I had noticed how neat he was about sharpening his knife and pencil. I said, "Are you the kind of man who when he peels an orange keeps the peeling all in one piece?"

"When I can." He rose from the table and took the wooden case and the can of oil to his bunk. When he came back, he said, "It looks like we could use some more firewood. I'll bring some in." He put on his hat and coat and went outside.

The boss was still working with the cloth and the saddle soap. When Dunbar was well outside, he said, "He must spend some of his spare time reading books."

"He has mentioned it to me on two or three occasions. I've tried to imagine him going back to New Jersey to spend his winters reading Charles Dickens and William Shakespeare, but it seems just as likely that he would go off to the frozen North and read ancient poems about Norsemen."

"Doesn't do any harm, I suppose. Reading books on his own time. He seems like a good enough cowpuncher, and that's what he says he is, but with some men, you never know everything about them."

---

THE BOSS SAT up straight after pushing away his breakfast plate. When he had the men's attention, he said, "We're going to build a foundation out of rocks and cement, cover it with canvas, and let it dry for a day or two before we build walls onto it. Just so you know, we'll be working with rocks and cement today. If you've got an old pair of gloves, you might want to wear them."

The new man went to his bunk and took out his pasteboard valise. He left his sheepskin coat on the foot of his bunk with the black hat on top of it, and he came back wearing a grey cloth cap and a drab shirt with three buttons and no pockets.

He told the boss he could mix cement, so he was busy at that task when I went out to observe the work at midmorning. He was turning over the wet, grey, cold-looking mush in a wooden trough called a boat.

The men had been bringing in rocks over the last few days, and they had accumulated a good-sized pile of them. The pile had gone down this morning, as the men were placing rocks along the string line where the boss had laid out the foundation. I stood by the boss and kept out of the way.

"So this is how big it's going to be," I said.

"That's right. Sixteen by twenty-four. These walls are going to be heavy, and we'll need all hands to raise them."

"I'll be glad to help," I said.

The sun shed its faint warmth on us. The boss was watching his project take shape, and I appreciated his optimism. He was not just a gatherer of stones but a builder in his small way. He had bought this ranch, had put together some capital, and was improving what he had. Not everyone could make a living off the land. For various reasons, people gave up and either went back or went on.

Wes Galvin was at a good point in life, in that middle period when a person has experience and confidence and can still see years stretching ahead. In other places, out on this autumn range, people my age and older were pulling together their forces in order to make it through the final stages. I glanced at the four workmen, all engaged in their labor, and I reflected on a thought I had had often since my mid-forties, when friends my age began to die. Each of us gets one chance at life, and none of us know how long we have.

The crew put in half the foundation the first day. As the sun went down, the men covered the work with canvas to hold in some of the warmth overnight. The sun sank fast at the end, but the colors lingered in the sky, with the yellow turning to orange and in some places scarlet like the blush of a peach. Narrow layers of clouds turned dark grey. I thought it would be a good evening for the hoot of the owl, but the bird did not come around while humans were milling about, talking, and clanking shovels.

---

Fair weather continued the next day, and the foundation was complete by midafternoon. The boss said the hands could work with horses and come back to cover up at the end of the day.

The sun's warmth felt fragile as it does at that time of year, but Partner was solid and warm to the touch. I brushed his coat and combed his mane and tail.

Dunbar was currying his own two horses, and Tyler was working with a smoke-colored horse. Ned Hacker was brushing a sorrel that had a white splash on its hip. He asked the new man, Deke, if he would like to ride.

Deke was wearing his hat and his sheepskin coat. In his smooth voice, he said, "It's been a while since I rode, but I could give it a try."

I had learned long ago to keep plenty of distance when two or more men were working with horses. With two on one horse, I gave them a little more room.

Hacker had a bridle on the horse as men often do when they are going to ride right away. He handed the reins to Deke and went for a saddle. He came bowlegging out of the barn with stirrups swinging as he carried a saddle and a blanket. Holding the saddle by the horn with his right hand, he spread the blanket on the horse's back with his free hand and swung the saddle up into place. Hacker had taken the rear cinch off his own saddle when he was not roping, but this saddle had a rear cinch on it. I realized it was Kent Norland's saddle. Hacker flipped the stirrup up out of the way, secured both cinches, and let the stirrup down.

"Go ahead," he said.

"Well, let's see." Deke set the reins and fiddled with the stirrup. He was taller than Hacker, but being out of practice, he had to lift his leg with his hand. He repositioned his hands on the rein and saddle horn and pulled himself up. The horse flinched as he swung his leg down on the other side and sank into the saddle.

"Have you got it?" asked Hacker.

"Sure. I'm fine."

The horse began to shift, so Deke pulled back on the reins with both hands and made a clicking sound with the corner of his mouth tucked back. The horse stutter-stepped, reared up, and showed its wide belly as it went over.

I felt a sick turn in my stomach as I heard the horse and man thud on the ground. The horse kicked and scrambled, pushed itself up, and trotted away with the stirrups flapping.

I dropped the rope to my horse and ran to look after the man. I bent over next to Ned Hacker, who stood close, and I said, "Are you all right?"

Deke stared up at me. His hat had fallen away, and he had bits of grass in his hair. "I think so."

"Can you stand up?"

"Let me see."

We helped him to his feet, but he was not steady. Hacker and I walked him to the bunkhouse as Tyler took care of our horses.

I thought he might die that night, but he didn't. I knew what it was like to be shaken up inside. In my own case, I found out there had been internal bleeding, and my body had to pass it out in more than one way. As Deke described the feeling of filling up and not being able to get rid of it, I thought I had an idea of what ailed him. But I was not a doctor, so I did not presume to tell him. I knew to have him drink water and to keep him covered with a blanket.

The boss said he was going to send some of us into town for lumber in the morning, and Deke could go if he wanted. Deke said he thought he might like that.

---

In the morning, Deke said he was so stiff he couldn't move, but we helped him to his feet and to the breakfast table. He said he could not eat but he could try some coffee. He shivered and trembled, but he drank a cup by himself.

When the boss asked him if he wanted to go to town, he said he did, and he would like his pay if he could have it. The boss said he had two dollars and a half coming but he was going to give him three for good measure.

Dunbar and I rode on the wagon seat, and Deke lay in back, covered with a couple of blankets. Ned Hacker rode alongside. From time to time, I looked back and asked Deke how he was doing. He would say that he hurt like hell and was cold.

In town, he said he would put up at the hotel and send for the doctor. With a smile, he said, "When we left the ranch, I thought that if I died, at least I wouldn't die broke. Now I'm not so sure."

We helped him out of the wagon, and to my surprise, he was able to walk with our help. Dunbar carried his pasteboard suitcase.

Inside the lobby, Deke mustered his best voice and said, "Thanks, fellas. If I make it out of this town, and if you're ever in Oak Hill, Texas, look me up. I'll return the favor."

"Take care of yourself," I said. "I took a bad fall from a horse one time, and it took me quite a while to get back to normal. I think you can do it."

"I wish you the best," said Dunbar.

Ned Hacker was standing with his horse by the wagon when we returned. He shook his head and said, "That's bad luck for you. You gotta wonder if it comes from sleepin' in Kent's blankets and usin' his saddle."

I thought he might as well blame the owl. I said, "He made it through the first night, and he's on his feet, even if he's shaky. I wouldn't say that he deserved it, although I don't know what he was doing with the reins, and I don't want to speak for him, but one way of looking at it is that he's luckier than some have been."

# 9

We found the lumberyard blocked by a string of three freight wagons with lumber to be unloaded. I knew that most of the lumber came from a sawmill up north and took more than a week in transport, so the appearance of this caravan was an important event. The owner of the lumberyard, a man named Campbell who had a bulbous red nose, asked me if we could come back in a few hours, say at one o'clock or so. I didn't see much choice, so I said it would be all right.

I turned the wagon around and headed toward the three-block area that made up the main part of town. Ned Hacker poked alongside on horseback.

"Seen the deppity go into the livery stable," he said.

"I noticed it, too," said Dunbar. "I also saw him in the dining room of the hotel when we were in there."

"Takes his own time to git around to doin' things."

Dunbar said, "I don't know how he works. But if he's still around, it means he's doing something. Sometimes a lawman can wear people down by keeping at it, coming back, and always asking questions."

"If he's goin' to the livery, that tells me he's goin' out somewhere."

"Sometimes they have to turn over a few rocks to find a worm."

I drove to the mercantile store. I was curious to see if Vivian was still working there, and the boss had told me to ask about an order.

The three of us walked down the center aisle of the store. Ned Hacker was making enough noise for all of us, taking roundabout strides and clunking his bootheels so that his spurs jingled. He had his thumbs in his belt, and his hat was tipped to one side.

An unfamiliar figure came out of the back room and stood behind the counter. It took me a couple of seconds to be sure I did not know him. He was lean and above average height, with a pale complexion, dark hair, beady eyes, and a shadow of a beard that looked like he had to shave twice a day. As our small group drew closer, I saw that he had a prominent Adam's apple and lips with a red tinge.

"What can I do for you?" he asked.

"I came to ask Mr. Fell about an order."

"I'll tell him." The man turned on his heel, walked through the open doorway, and spoke a few words. My eyes drifted upward to the hawk on the perch. The clerk came out and said, "He'll be right here." He stood up off his heels, settled, and stared at us in silence.

I took a casual glance at him. He wore an ash-grey shirt with an open neck, a dull black gabardine coat with grey metal buttons and a close military-style fit, and creased pants to match. His polished black boots had round toes and one-inch heels, a style I had seen on church choir directors when I was a boy.

Fell came out of the back room at a fast walk and slowed when he came into our view. He showed his teeth as he smiled.

"Mr. Ryerson. I didn't expect to see you again so soon."

"We're in town today to pick up lumber. The boss told me that while I was at it, I could drop in and see if by any chance his order has come in."

He brushed with his finger at his trimmed mustache. "I remember what it was. Two kerosene lamps, a set of door hinges, a door latch, and a block and tackle. I ordered it all together, to save him money, and it should all arrive at the same time. If it comes at such a time as when I think you might not be in for a few days, like at the beginning of the week, I would be happy to run it out to you or to have someone else deliver it."

As if he had all the time in the world right now, he took out a penknife, which must have been sharp, and cut a thread off the side of his jacket. He slipped the knife back into his pocket.

"Don't go to any extra trouble," I said. "We just dropped in to ask because we were in town anyway."

"Of course." Fell drew himself up, and from the motion he made with his hand, I thought he was going to take out his cigarette case. Instead, he gave a short cough into his fist. "By the way, this is my new clerk. 'Erman." He coughed again.

I was not sure that I heard right. "Ermine?" I asked.

"Herman," said the clerk, pushing the *H*.

Fell spoke in a more energetic tone. "This is Mr. Ryerson. He runs the bunkhouse out at the Hook ranch, and these are a couple of his hired hands."

I did not care for the way he presented me as if I were a foreman, but I did not want to make more of it by making a correction. "Pleased to meet you," I said.

"Same here," said the clerk.

Fell now brought out his cigarette case with the gold-stitched diamond pattern, but before opening it, he glared at Ned Hacker, who was craning his neck to look through the open doorway to the back room. In a curt voice, Fell said, "Whatever you're looking for, it isn't here."

Hacker raised his chin, and his words came out like gravel. "How do you know what I'm lookin' for?"

Fell's eyes were keen. "I don't need to." He turned to me, and his face relaxed. "Is there anything else we can help you with today?"

"I don't think so." I had already surmised that Vivian was no longer working there, and I imagined that he thought I already knew.

"Thanks for dropping in, then." Fell turned to his left, and with a drop in his voice, he said, "We don't need anything. You can go back to what you were doing."

Alan, the errand boy, was keeping his distance at the edge of our gathering. I nodded to him, took leave of the owner and the new clerk, and left with my two fellow workers behind me.

Outside, the sun was shining but a breeze was blowing. I wondered how the cement was curing out at the ranch.

I said to Dunbar, "I think we have time to go to the LaSalle." I turned to Hacker. "How about you?"

"I can find something to do."

I had brought cold meat and biscuits, thinking we would eat on the way home. With our change in schedule, I said, "How about meeting us in front of the lumberyard at noon? We can eat our lunch and see how soon we can expect to load our order."

"Suits me."

Dunbar and I climbed into the wagon, and I set the horses into motion. The café was only a block away, but I did not want to leave the wagon in front of the mercantile. I felt that I was being a bit peevish in knowing where I might find Vivian while I left Ned Hacker to wonder, but I figured he had time enough to find out for himself.

The LaSalle Café did not have any customers, but the interior was warm and well lit. Mrs. Deville and Vivian were arranging plates and cups and bowls in the shelves in back of the counter. They turned around at the sound of the doorbell, and they both smiled.

"We're getting closer," said Mrs. Deville.

Vivian's cheeks showed good color, and her eyes were bright. "Good morning to both of you. It's not yet noon, is it?"

"Not by quite a bit," I said. "It's good to see you here."

"Good to be here."

"We stopped in at the mercantile and met the new clerk."

She winced. "I've seen him. He has even passed by here on his walk."

A rattle of dishes sounded in the kitchen, and I

guessed that someone was working in there as well. Dunbar and I had taken off our hats, and I felt idle as we stood there.

"Don't let us keep you from your work," I said.

"Quite all right," said Mrs. Deville as she walked to the kitchen.

Dunbar stood aside, and I was left a few feet from Vivian.

"It looks like you're doing all right," I said. "I hope you didn't have any trouble getting away from the other place."

"Not much at all. More my own nervousness than anything else. But there was something that happened that I think I should tell you about."

"Oh." I weighed my thoughts for a moment. "We came to town to pick up some lumber. We're supposed to meet at the lumberyard at noon, where we can eat a lunch I brought along and then see when we can have the lumber."

"I see. Then you go back to the ranch."

"That's the plan right now."

"Let me see if Medora will let me have a few minutes."

"Mrs. Deville?"

"She has us call her by her first name."

I waited apart from Dunbar as Vivian went into the kitchen.

She came out a minute later and said, "It's all right. Let's go out front. Not many people come down this way yet, and I can watch to see if somebody is within hearing distance."

I followed her outside onto the sidewalk, where the sun reflected off the building and the breeze was blocked off. I hoped she was not in any difficulties, but I waited for her to speak.

After looking up and down the street to be sure we were alone, she said, "Mr. Fell came to see me the second day I was working here. Yesterday. I thought at first that he wanted to ask me to come back to work for him, but he assured me right away that that wasn't his purpose. He said he needed to talk to me about something else, but he needed to talk to me alone. I told him that if we could stand out here in plain view, I would talk to him."

She looked up and down the street again, and I nodded for her to go on.

"He threw himself at my feet—just in a manner of speaking, of course. For the first time, I did not feel afraid of him. I don't think I need to repeat the whole conversation, but the short of it is that I turned him down."

"Whew."

"He didn't like it. I think he felt he had gone far enough, or farther than he intended, and he became indignant. He told me it was no small offer, that not just any old girl could expect to hear it. Then I began to feel again that there was something about him to be afraid of. But all of this was in plain daylight, and he got hold of himself again and smiled and thanked me for listening to him. But I didn't go home alone. Medora and I go back and forth together, though sometimes she works here by herself or with Madeline."

"And how do you get along with her—the kitchen girl?"

"Well enough, so far."

"I ask because I'm a bit worried about you being in

contact with someone who is, to put it in polite terms, less innocent in the ways of the world."

"I think I know what you mean. She's polite and well-intentioned, but she's not very refined. But I take her at her word that she's trying to improve her life."

"Yes, and I didn't mean to . . . disparage her. I know she means well, and she has a little girl to take care of."

"I know that from before. Alan told me. By the way, did you see him when you stopped at the store?"

"Yes, I did. His boss seems to treat him as always."

"Poor boy. I feel guilty for leaving him there by himself, and now with this odious clerk. But I had to get out when I could."

"You did well, and I hope there aren't any other repercussions."

"So do I." She glanced up and down the street. "Well, this has been at least a few minutes. I should get back to work."

"Yes, and you don't want to catch cold. It's not as warm out here as it feels like at first."

"I'm not cold, but I should go in, anyway."

Dunbar was standing by himself, hat in hand, when we walked inside. I took off my hat and stood near him. Vivian went back to her work, and Mrs. Deville came out of the kitchen. She signaled to Dunbar and to me, and we moved toward her and stood together.

"I have a little favor to ask," she began. "I think it would be better if the two of you are there, not that either of you couldn't do it alone. There's a fellow who comes around the back door and pesters Madeline. I would like someone to tell him to go away and not hang around the back door or in back of the building.

I think he's less likely to put up a fight if there are two people there."

I had a hunch about who it might be, and Dunbar gave me a knowing look with his eyebrows raised.

"We might as well," I said.

We put on our hats and went outside to meet Critter, who backed up into the sunlight. I saw that his short-billed cap was made of leather. He had long, dirty-looking brown hair with a matching beard. Beneath his coat, a buttonless leather vest hung loose over a khaki shirt, and his canvas trousers looked as if they had once belonged to a larger man. On his hip, he wore a knife in a scabbard that had a leather thong hanging from the tip.

Dunbar had taken the lead, so Critter faced him.

"Who are you?"

"The person who's telling you to move along. My name's Dunbar, but it shouldn't make a difference."

"It don't."

"The person who has this business has asked me to tell you not to hang around. So I'm telling you."

"You can't tell me what to do."

"I *am* telling you. Don't be a nuisance to other people."

The man's yellowish-brown eyes narrowed. "She's mine."

Dunbar's features became rigid. "I'm talking on behalf of the person who has this business, but I will tell you this, citizen. No one is another person's property. You've been told to move on. If you don't, the next step is to send for the law."

Critter looked him up and down, cast his narrow eyes over me, and pivoted in the gravel. "We're not done yet," he said, and he stalked away as before, in his forward-leaning posture.

---

WE DROVE the wagon to the lumberyard and met Hacker for a cold lunch. He did not ask us what we had done, and neither of us asked him. When we finished eating, he asked what time it was. I took out my watch and showed him a quarter past twelve.

He said, "We've got plenty of time. One beer won't hurt. The way we've been put off, we won't have time for one later."

Although I still did not care for the way Fell had built me up, I was in charge on a little excursion such as this one. "I suppose," I said, "but I don't want to keep anyone else waiting."

We left the wagon on the side of the street and walked a short distance east to the corner. We stayed on the north side of the street as we walked another half-block to the saloon. The front door was closed but not locked, so we walked in. Daylight appeared on the inside and then faded as Hacker closed the door behind us.

We took our places at the bar, which ran along the right wall. Lamps were lit above the bar as they were at night, but the area above the tables and the piano remained unlit. Only two other customers were present, and they were talking to one another in low voices at the far end of the bar.

Dunbar called for three mugs of beer and paid for them.

Hacker said, "It was my idea to come here. I could have paid."

"Not anything to worry about." Dunbar stood sideways to the bar, in a position where he could keep an eye on the door.

Hacker rolled a cigarette and lit it. He shook out the match, dropped it at his feet, and stepped on it. He spoke in his rough voice. "I didn't like the way that storekeeper acted when we were in there. Eagle-beak son of a bitch. Always out to prove somethin', like he's better than you are." Hacker squinted as he took another drag. "Reminds me of a big bug back home. He had a wagon shop and always had two or three stiffs workin' for him. He had a daughter, and she wouldn't look at the likes of me if I saw her on the street, even though I was in school with her the first three years."

I had heard some of this before, and it was connected with his larger idea that the people who had money never gave a fair chance to those who didn't.

He went on. "I told her one time, when I was little, that I wanted to raise my own horses when I got older. She just looked at me with her eyes bugged out. Someday I'll go back there."

The door opened, and daylight spilled in as a man stood in the doorway and surveyed the inside. I could not recognize him until he moved inside and let the door close behind him. He was the round-shouldered lout in the bowler hat. He was wearing his dark overcoat, and he walked with a bouncy step and his hands hanging straight down. He angled to the end of the bar closest to the door and slapped a coin on the bar top.

"Just a glass of beer," he called out.

I remembered that he drank whiskey the other two times I saw him, and I wondered if he was the type who drank beer through the first part of the day and moved up.

The bartender served him a mug of beer. He drank about a third of it and let out a long *Aahh!* sound.

"Just get up?" asked the bartender.

"You think. You should have seen the pork chop I had for breakfast."

The bartender took the coin and swiped his rag on the bar. "I can imagine."

The man finished his beer before long and made his sound of satisfaction as he thumped the empty mug on the bar top. I stared up at the stuffed eagle to keep from looking at him, but he was hard to ignore.

When he had walked out and the door had closed behind him, I asked Hacker if he knew the man.

"Oh, yeah. His name's Cage. He works at the Blue Diamond."

I exchanged a glance with Dunbar.

Hacker went on. "He's just the doorman, but he'd like you to think he's got the pick of the litter."

Dunbar said, "He has a famous bow up at the castle."

"What's that?" I asked.

"It's an old saying, based on an old story about a man who drinks in a tavern down in the village. He tells the villagers that he lives up in the castle and has a famous bow there, from some ancient battle. All of the villagers are common folk, and they can't go up to the castle to find out, but the likelihood is that he minds the gate, lights torches, and feeds the dogs."

Hacker said, "Well, I've been to that whorehouse, and that's about the way it is. He ain't nothin' special."

The door opened again, and a shorter, wider form

moved out of the shadow with the bright light behind. I did not find it difficult to recognize Thad Coulter as he came toward us in his rocking shuffle, tapping his tall cane on the floor.

"Well, well, if it isn't the Hook boys. Takin' your lunch?"

"Washing it down," I said. "How about yourself? Out making your rounds?"

"Something like that." He came to a stop and breathed out hard through his nose. "I'm like an old turtle. Get out and move around while the sun's out. Anything new at the ranch?"

"Nothing big to speak of. The boss is building a feed shed, and he sent us in for materials."

"Hah. That's good. I thought I heard something like that. Been to Fell's?"

I had to pick his last words apart to understand the question. "Yes, we have," I said.

"What did you think of his new clerk, or did you see him?"

"Yes, I did, but I can't say I had any thoughts about him."

Coulter shifted from one foot to the other, signaled to the bartender, and heaved out another breath through his bushy mustache. "You can tell he's not from here. He reminds me of the Barber of Seville."

I frowned. "I don't know who that is."

"I saw the play one time, and this fellow here looks like the character in the play." Coulter reached for his beer and told the bartender to put it on his tab.

Dunbar said, "Isn't that an opera?"

Coulter nodded. "Oh, yeah. They sang all the way through." The beer touched his mustache as he bent and took a drink. He raised his heavy head, lowered his mug, and shifted on his feet to look at Hacker. "And how about you, young feller? What do you have to say for yourself?"

"Not much."

"I thought I recognized you earlier."

Hacker shrugged.

In his light way, as if he was talking about the weather, Coulter said, "Sorry about what happened to your *compadre*."

Hacker shrugged again. "Not much you can do about it."

"I guess not." Coulter turned to Dunbar. "And yourself?"

"Well enough, thanks."

"You're friends with the lady who came to town, aren't you? I hope she does well."

"Thanks."

I did not want Coulter to ask me about my niece in front of Hacker, so I asked him, "Where did you see that production about the Barber of Seville?"

"Oh, that was in Omaha. A long time ago. But you know how things stick with you. And I didn't understand half of it."

Hacker, Dunbar, and I finished our drinks, and I did not like to leave Coulter by himself in the saloon. I saw that he had put most of his beer away already, so I said, "We're about ready to go. If you're going to have another, we'll leave you here, but if not, we'll wait and go to the door with you."

"I just have one at this time of the day. Later on, give me a chair and let me light a cigar, and I'll have a couple." He chortled. "Even at that, I'm too old to get into trouble anymore."

The four of us walked to the door at a slow pace, with Hacker staying in back and taking his clunking steps. The daylight was bright when I stepped outside, as I expected, and I stood for a moment to let my eyes adjust and to see that Coulter made it through the doorway. When I brought my gaze around, I saw that Dunbar had stopped and was facing a man who blocked his way. I took a step to the right to see what was going on.

The walkway was dirt, with no board sidewalk, so the man at the edge of the street was on the same level as we were. He had his head tipped to one side, and the pale sunlight reflected on his leather cap. His name ran through my mind. *Critter.* He had his hands at his sides, and the leather thong dangled from the sheath of his knife. I did not think he looked dangerous, but I thought he wanted to look tough.

"What do you want?" said Dunbar.

Critter lolled his head. "I don't let some lubber tell me what I can do and where I can go."

Dunbar said, "I think you should move along and not start trouble."

Critter took a quick step forward and pushed with both hands on Dunbar's chest. "Don't' tell me what to do, fella. Make me move." He narrowed his yellowish-brown eyes and doubled his fist at his side.

"I'm telling you to get out of the way."

Critter raised his fist to swing, but he did not make it halfway when Dunbar punched him. He fell back a step and came forward, lifting his fist again. Dunbar hit him twice, with a right and a left, and he went down.

Dunbar waited as Critter came to his feet. His cap had fallen off, and he had it in his hand. He put it on his head with a tug, and without looking at Dunbar, he turned to his right and stalked away.

Thad Coulter stood tapping his cane in short, quick motions. "That's business," he said.

Dunbar shook his head. "Nothin' good."

I said to Coulter, "We're going this way, so we'll see you later."

"Sure," he said. "I just want to let that jaybird get a ways ahead of me."

## 10

I DID NOT SEE ANYONE MOVING AROUND IN THE lumberyard, so I waited until one o'clock straight up to walk in and ask. Campbell came out of the office and told me that his men had left for dinner a few minutes earlier. I agreed to come back in half an hour.

At the wagon, I shared the news with Dunbar and Hacker. I was afraid Hacker would want to go back into the saloon, so I said, "I don't think it would do to go into the Double Eagle again, but we have half an hour to kill. I think Dunbar and I could walk down to the café again, in case this troublemaker has gone there to be a nuisance with Mrs. Deville's scrub woman. You could stay here and watch the wagon and your horse, or if there's something you want to—"

"I can go over and visit at the blacksmith shop."

I knew Hacker was a restless sort and did not like to stay put. The blacksmith shop was across the wide main street and the next location west of the livery stable, and I recalled that one of the fellows who worked there was a pal of Hacker's.

"That should be all right," I said. "You can keep an eye on the wagon and horse while you're at it."

"Nothin' happened to 'em earlier."

I did not want to argue, so I said, "We'll be back in less than half an hour."

I thought the best place to find Critter was in the alley, but I did not want to cross paths with him behind the hotel or the mercantile, and I did not much care where he was as long as he was not pestering anyone at the café. I also did not want to walk past the front window of the mercantile, as we had done so not much more than an hour earlier. So I took us across the main street and proceeded along the south side for more than two blocks east until we came to the coal and drayage company. The front of the café was calm as we crossed the street toward it.

Inside, Mrs. Deville was standing on the counter near the wall. She had a hammer in her hand, and she looked at her feet as if to see whether she was displaying anything in an improper way.

"Just in time," she said to Dunbar. "You can pull this nail for me." She stepped down onto a chair behind the counter.

Dunbar took off his hat, stayed in a crouch as he climbed up, and pulled the nail that was driven into the wall about a foot from the ceiling. He set the hammer and the crooked nail on the counter as he climbed down.

Addressing both Mrs. Deville and Vivian, he said, "We had a little run-in with this fellow who has been annoying you. We had a few minutes on our hands, so we walked down here to see if he's come back. He seems like a persistent sort."

Mrs. Deville brushed at a loose hair on the side of her head. "I'll go see."

I heard her speak a few words to Madeline, unlatch the door, and latch it again. She returned to the front area and said, "No sign of anything at the moment."

"That's good," said Dunbar. "Like I said, we had a few minutes, so we thought we'd check. Is there anything else we can do while we're here?"

Mrs. Deville raised her eyebrows as she stood in a slight turn with her arms crossed in front of her. With her dark hair, white blouse, and dark skirt, she struck a lively pose.

"Why not?" she said. "Two big, strong men. You could put the chairs upside down on the tables so we can sweep and mop."

We finished the task in about five minutes. I took out my watch, put it away, and said, "I think it's time we started back."

Mrs. Deville and Vivian thanked us, and we left with the sound of the doorbell fading behind us.

The breeze from the northwest had picked up, and it was bringing grey clouds. We kept to the north side of the street, where there would be less wind, and we marched the three blocks to the wagon.

Hacker was nowhere in sight, so I hurried across to the blacksmith's shop to fetch him. I met his friend, a tall, lean fellow with hunched shoulders, prominent cheekbones, and dark teeth. He wore a skull cap and a leather apron, and his face was smudged. He said Hacker had dropped by to chin for a few minutes and had gone back to the wagon.

The lumberyard hands said they had not seen him. I assumed he would show up in a few minutes, so

Dunbar tied the saddle horse to a rail as I drove the wagon into the yard.

With so much of the day already gone and the wind bringing in the weather, Dunbar and I stacked the lumber in the wagon as fast as Campbell's two men could bring it to us. Still, I took the time to reject boards that I thought were too warped or split. Dunbar tied down the load while I went over the list, which Campbell called a bill of lading. The sun had gone out of sight, and I smelled moisture in the air as I stepped outside to join Dunbar.

"Still no sign of Ned?" I asked.

Dunbar shook his head.

"Damn it," I said. "If he's in the saloon, I'll have something to say to him. If you go get his horse, I'll pull this wagon out and around."

Dunbar had the horse tied in front of the Double Eagle by the time I drove up. "I'll go in and look for him if you want," he said.

"Go ahead." I took out my watch and saw that it was almost three-thirty. The sun would be starting to slip in another hour, and with the clouds, the light would go down even sooner. I had already seen that the lumber made a heavy load for only two horses, so we had a long, slow drive ahead of us.

Dunbar came out of the saloon with a quick step. "He's not there. They haven't seen him since he was in there earlier with us."

"They?"

"Sorry. He. All I spoke to was the bartender, although there were a couple of other chaps down the bar. Same ones as before."

"Damn. I wonder where he is."

"We know three places where he isn't. And he wouldn't have gone far without his horse."

I gazed at the brown horse with the single-rigged saddle and found no answer there. "I hope we don't have to ask in every place in town." I drummed my fingers on my knee. "It's been a long time."

Dunbar did not answer. I sensed that he did not want to irritate me.

"Well," I said, "the barbershop is two doors down. I can ask in there if anyone has seen him, and you can go across to the post office. Those are the two lookouts. If they haven't seen him, it would be hard to guess who has."

"I'll do that." Dunbar set off across the street.

As I climbed down from the seat, I touched the iron rail on the side and felt the cold. I put on my gloves as I headed for the barbershop.

Jake Steck, the barber, jumped up out of his chair and stood waiting. "What'll it be, Rye?"

"Nothing for me, Jake, but thanks. I'm looking for one of the hired hands that came in with us today. Ned Hacker. Not very tall, reddish-brown hair, kind of a ruddy complexion." I moved my hand in front of my face.

"I know who you mean. I haven't seen him. I saw you and the taller one walk by a couple of times, but that was more than two hours ago. Well, you know when that was." Jake's eyes went past me and came back. "Anything wrong?"

"I don't know. He was supposed to wait for us to load some lumber, and I don't know where he went."

"Try the saloon."

"We did. He's not there."

"Maybe he went to eat at the hotel. Then there's that new café, but I don't think it's open yet. Well, I guess you know that, too."

"We ate our lunch at the wagon. And he's been missing for over two hours. Even if he went to eat something more, he wouldn't be gone that long."

Jake put his hands in the pockets of his white barber's shirt. "I don't know what to tell you, Rye."

"Thanks all the same."

"Maybe one other thing."

"What's that?"

"You know how these young fellas are. He might be laid up with a girl somewhere."

I tensed. "Not very likely. He was waiting to go back to work with us, as soon as the lumberyard hands came back from dinner. But thanks."

"Glad to help. If I can do anything else, let me know."

"Well, we're looking for him. The more who know about it, the better, I guess." I did not like to feed the town gossip, but I felt the day slipping away.

"Sure. I'll mention it if I happen to see anyone."

I went outside and stood by the wagon as Dunbar came across the street from the post office.

"No luck," I said. "The barber knows who Ned is, but he hasn't seen him. He saw us, of course, and was happy to report that."

"Same with the postmaster."

"The barber said he might be laid up with a girl. I said I didn't think it was very likely because he was waiting to go to work. The road ranch is a good five miles away, and he seemed to know about it, but he was on foot. I wouldn't know where to look in town, even if he fell into something."

Dunbar said, "Not to put too fine a point on it, the one possibility we might know about is busy scrubbing the kitchen. And if we take her word for it, she's not looking for that kind of work now, anyway. It seems to be pursuing her as she tries to get away from it."

"I think we can rule out that part, then. The only other thing I can imagine, along those lines, and I don't like to mention it in the same breath, is that he might have wanted to know where my niece is. We didn't see a trace of him either time at the café, but he may not know she's there." I recalled him stretching his neck to look into the back room of the mercantile. "Even at that, it's been hours now. I don't want to ask in every place in town, but I don't know if we should go back to the ranch without him."

"That's the way it is when someone goes missing. I think we should get more people to look for him. The word will spread, too."

"I think you're right," I said. "I wonder where we should start."

"We can go to the hotel and see if the deputy has come back in for the day."

The Arcade Hotel was the second business farther down the street on our side. I could see the high front from where I stood. "That's a good idea," I said. "It could save us time."

The deputy came down from his room, carrying his hat in his hand. His badge caught the lamplight, and his pistol rode on his hip. He held his small brown eyes on me and rubbed his recessed chin as he listened to my story.

"It's hard to say he's gone missing if it's just been a few hours," he said.

"Yes, but he was supposed to go to work, and he

couldn't have wandered far. He left his horse. That is, a ranch horse, but it has his saddle."

"He could be passed out somewhere."

"He drank one glass, or mug, of beer and didn't go back into the saloon."

"He may have passed out from something else. He might have gotten dizzy and sat down in the alley somewhere."

"If that's the case, we need to find him. Sundown is on the way, and the temperature is going down. If something worse has happened, we need to—"

"What reason would anyone have to do something to him?"

"I have no idea. I don't know that anyone did. But I know he's missing."

The deputy's narrow chest went up and down as he took a slow breath. Without his hat and coat, standing in his tan-and-yellow flannel shirt and brown cloth vest, he looked soft in the stomach. He blinked his eyes and said, "I guess we can try."

Dunbar and I waited outside. The minutes dragged. No one appeared or moved on the street. At last, Deputy Caryl came out of the hotel, wearing his hat, his lined canvas coat, and his leather gloves. He stopped a few feet from us and put his hands in his coat pockets.

"It's better to do this in an organized way. Not have people scattered all over. We have to get the people together first. I'll take this side of the street, and you can take the other side." He settled his eyes on me. "Everyone knows you, so you can do the talking. In each place, ask if someone from there can come and join a search party. Ask them to tell anyone else they know. But it's going to get dark, so we don't need any kids to get lost or women to worry about. Just men will be best."

"Where do you want people to go? Where do we start?"

The deputy twisted his mouth. "Where was he seen last?"

"At the wagon when it was in front of the lumberyard. And at the blacksmith shop across the street, just before that." I waved my hand in that direction. "They're both at the edge of town."

"Then we can start there. Tell everyone to meet there in twenty minutes."

Again I felt time slipping away. "That means we can't get started until twenty minutes after the last person has been told."

The deputy took his hands out of his pockets and pressed them together with his gloved fingers interlocking. "It's common to plan these for the next day. I still don't know he's lost. I'm tryin' to accommodate you."

"All right." I turned to Dunbar. "How would you like to take the wagon and the horse back to there? If that's our starting point, it may be our finishing point."

"Sure," he said.

"I'll start at the bank, then, and I'll catch the livery stable and the blacksmith shop when I get back to you."

"Very good. And I'll keep an eye out, of course."

I checked my watch. It showed a few minutes until four. I took off at a fast walk.

As I went into one business after another, I had the curious sensation of being shuttled back and forth in time. Almost every business had a clock in view, and there was no consistency or continuity. Time would jump ahead and fall back. When I finished the last business on my side, which was the coal and drayage company, the sky had not changed much. When I reached the wagon after my dead march in return and a stop in two places, a small crowd of men had gathered. My watch showed half past four.

At length the deputy arrived. He asked Dunbar to hold the horses, and he climbed up into the front of the wagon to face the crowd. Voices died down. The deputy spoke in a calm tone and not very loud.

"Folks, as you know, we think someone needs to be found. He's been missin' for a few hours now, and it's about to get dark. We want to spread out and make a clean sweep from west to east. We're pretty sure he's not anywhere on Main Street itself, so we'll start in the alleyway on each side and spread out to cover two blocks. When we get to the other end, if we haven't found anything by then, we'll turn around and pick up anything on the edges on the way back. Let's not anyone be in a hurry."

The crowd dispersed, and men spoke to one another as they spread out. A couple of men on each side had lanterns. I took the same side of the street I had gone down earlier, and the deputy took the north side. Dunbar went with that group as well. A man in my group had a speckled spaniel, and I soon learned that its name was Jip.

I worked the alley with two other men, one of whom had a lantern with a shade that directed a beam of light outward. We moved in and out of the shadows as night fell. Dogs barked. A couple of people from the houses on the right side came out to see what was going on. They had not heard the news yet. Now and then, a cat started up and dashed away.

When we reached the east edge of town, people lingered. I heard that the deputy wanted to wait until everyone made the first pass, and we could all start back at the same time.

Night had closed in. Men were chatting. Some were walking around in the way men do to stay warm, and a couple of cigarette ends glowed in the dark. The spaniel was running back and forth, and its owner was calling its name.

Without any warning, a cry went up on the north side, followed by calls of "Found something" and "Over here." Everyone rushed, and the figures seemed to dance as lanterns swung. Things came to a stop a hundred yards out from the last house on the north side of the alley. Dunbar reached the edge of the small crowd just as I did. At that moment, someone farther in said, "It's him."

"Let me see," I said. "Let me see." I pushed my way through and stopped short where the body of a man lay in the short, dry grass. Two lanterns cast more than enough light for me to recognize him by his ruddy complexion and reddish-brown hair. He was wearing the brown coat with wooden buttons that he was wearing earlier in the day, and his hat was lying near his outstretched hand.

I began to speak, and I had to push down the lump in my throat. "That's him," I said. "That's Ned Hacker."

A person brushed against my elbow, and I saw that it was the deputy. "I need to take over here," he said. He knelt by the body and touched a bare finger to the man's neck. "He's cold, and I don't feel a pulse. We'll need a wagon or a cart or something like that."

I said, "Our wagon is at the other end of town, and it has a load of lumber on it."

"Anything will do," said the deputy. "But you can stay with me until we get him to the coroner's."

I took him to mean the barber. "Of course."

"We'll look him over in better light, but right now I don't see any blood or a head wound." The deputy stood up and spoke in a louder voice. "Anyone who wants to can go home. We thank you all for your help. Things go better when everyone works together. I need someone to volunteer a wagon, though."

The man from the livery stable was holding a lantern. He said, "I can do that as easy as anyone. I'll be right back."

The postmaster held the other lantern. He said, "I'd stay with this light, but I came without a coat."

Dunbar said, "I can hold it. We'll make sure it gets back to you."

The postmaster moved his eyes from Dunbar to the deputy to me. "All right," he said. He handed Dunbar the lantern and hurried away.

---

IN THE WELL-LIT back room of the barbershop, Ned Hacker's body lay face-up on a canvas sheet with his coat open and laid back on both sides. Dunbar stood back, and I looked aside, as the deputy pulled garments up and down and ran his hands into pockets.

"I still don't see any blood. No knife or bullet wounds. No evidence of a blow on the head. Here's what he had on him." The deputy motioned with his left hand at a few articles lying next to the body on the canvas sheet. I saw a small leather wallet, a few coins including two five-dollar gold pieces, and the dead man's clasp knife. It had a small, nickel-plated diamond set into the wood handle.

"And this," said the deputy. He opened his right hand, and in his palm he held a silver watch and a key.

My mind jumped and came back as I stared at the object. "That's Kent Norland's watch," I said.

"I thought it might be, from the description you gave the other day."

"I don't know why Ned would have it on him. He didn't carry a watch, and he had to ask me for the time when we were eating lunch."

The deputy, still calm, said, "And as I recall, this fella here mentioned the watch when we found the other man's body. I don't think he would have done that if he had had it on him."

I exchanged a glance with Dunbar. I said, "This seems too obvious. Someone put this watch on him to make it seem as if he did in Kent Norland out of jealousy."

"All we have is the facts," said the deputy. "And you know how fond people are of sayin' that the facts speak for themselves. Which of course they don't. But I think that if all we do is state the facts of what we found, and keep the theory out of it, we might have a better chance of learnin' more."

The barber had been standing back all this time, but I was sure he did not miss anything. He said, "So you mean to say—"

"What I mean to say is that we found the other man's watch on him. That's all. This is still an open investigation, and to the extent that you receive a coroner's fee, you don't need to say anything more than that."

"Oh, I know how to keep mum," said the barber.

"So do we," I said. I was telling the truth so well that I almost felt guilty for not telling anyone else about the diamond-and-emerald pendant. I was sure that whoever had had Kent Norland's watch still had the pendant. But I did not know it for a fact, so I kept the theory to myself.

Outside, Dunbar and I agreed that we should check on the women at the café, if they were still there. We walked along the dark street without talking, and I imagined he was lapsing into his own thoughts as I was doing with mine.

Up until this moment, the death of Ned Hacker had been a plain reality we had to deal with, sort of a cold fact in itself. Now with the practical tasks taken care of and the disciplined part of me not having to hold things down, I had a mixture of feelings rising up within me. Even though I had never cared all that much for the victim, I was pondering again the death of a young person who had lost the chance to do as much as he could with his life. I recalled my conversation with Mrs. Williams and our recognition that when a young person dies, it is someone's family member. I was used to people saying that they lost a relative such as a parent or child, that the person had been taken from them. I was sure it was a natural response. But I had also arrived at the idea on my own that the person who lost the most was the deceased.

I recalled the likes of Thad Coulter, who could be matter-of-fact about anyone else's death, and I thought that was natural, too. So it might be with any of the men who joined the search party. Even in a small town, there would be people who had to worry about their shortness of breath, excessive weight, or bad habits catching up with them.

"Looks like someone's there," said Dunbar.

My thoughts came back to the moment as I saw light shining out of the café window.

The door was locked, but Mrs. Deville let us in. "We're making plans to go home," she said. She stood in the center of the room as we walked in and took off our hats.

Alan James, the errand boy, was sitting at a table with Vivian. Noise from the kitchen told me that someone was keeping busy there.

"We've heard the news," said Mrs. Deville. "We had seen the search party earlier, so we knew something was afoot."

Vivian had moist eyes but looked as if she was bearing up. Alan had his hands folded together in front of him on the table, and I interpreted that he had come to offer whatever support he could. I imagined he might have brought the news as well.

I met his eyes and said, "I didn't see anyone from the store in the search party."

Alan shook his head. "Herman had already left for the day. Mr. Fell said he couldn't leave the store alone. And he had work for me to do."

I nodded and addressed Vivian and Mrs. Deville. "We came on foot. Our wagon is at the other end of town with a load of lumber, and we have yet to go to the ranch. But we can see you people to your residences on our way from here."

"That would be most kind," said Mrs. Deville.

A coughing sound from the door to the kitchen caught her attention. She walked to the doorway, and after a muffled conversation with Madeline, she came back to face Dunbar and me.

"Before we go, Madeline would like to speak to the two of you for a minute. If you don't mind."

"Not at all," said Dunbar, stepping forward and then stopping. "I suppose I shouldn't speak for you."

"I'm with you," I said.

In the kitchen, Madeline held her green eyes on us. Her dusky face was clean, and her dark hair was tied back. She wore a long, dark grey work dress with an apron of lighter grey over it.

"I heard what happened," she said. "I think I should tell you something I know, for the same reasons I said before. It's not much, and I don't want to take up too much of your time, but—"

"We have time," I said.

Her eyes went to the doorway. "I'd rather talk outside, if you don't mind. I don't mean anything about any of them, but I think it would be better."

"We don't mind," I said. I glanced at Dunbar for confirmation, and we followed her to the door. She picked up her hooded coat on the way, turned the latch, and led the way out into the dark night. I closed the door behind us. When we were all three standing in place, she let out a shuddering breath and began.

"None of this is easy to talk about, but like I said before, I think someone should know." She paused and moistened her lips. "This fella who just died, I don't think it would surprise you to know that I knew him." She paused. "I knew him like I knew the other one, in a business kind of way. Just not as much."

I said, "Did you happen to see him earlier today?"

"Oh, no. I would say it's been more than two weeks since I even talked to him."

"Go ahead. I'm sorry to interrupt you."

"I don't mind." She took in both of us with her eyes. "Whatever happened today doesn't have anything to do with me. Or I sure hope it doesn't. But the part I wanted to tell you has to do with both of them, and now that they're both dead, it feels strange. But anyway, this fella Ned was jealous of the other one, because of the girl they both liked."

She said the last few words with such care that I understood why she wanted to speak outside.

"Go ahead," I said.

"So Ned knew that the other one came to me and did things with me, and even though he did, too, he thought it was low-down that the other one did while he was supposed to care so much about a girl. I don't think he saw that the same thing could be said about him. Anyway, he knew about it, and he threatened to tell on him. To the girl."

She paused as if to let me speak, but I had the presence of mind to keep my thoughts to myself. All of my recent sympathies for Ned Hacker vanished for the moment, and I was appalled by his hypocrisy as well as by the thought that he would share that kind of information with a decent girl or that he would threaten to. I shook my head.

Madeline went on. "Like I told you before, the first one used to tell me that he felt guilty and tried to stay away, and then he would weaken to the temptation and feel guilty all over again. Then he felt worse when Ned threatened to tell on him. But here's the reason I wanted to talk to you." She turned to Dunbar to include him as before. "They say they found the first one's watch on Ned, which would make someone think he took it when he killed him. Out of jealousy. But it doesn't make sense. If anyone had a reason, it was Kent. People kill people who try to blackmail them. But he didn't have it in him to do something like that, and he knew he was wrong in the first place to try to be something he wasn't. But he wanted to be. He wanted to be better than he was. And I felt sorry for him, because I know what it's like. Ned didn't have any of that in him. Oh, maybe he wanted to be better, but he didn't have any remorse for the mean things he did or threatened to do."

Dunbar said, "And to get back to the main point, he didn't have any motive to kill Kent Norland and take his watch."

"No, and that *is* the main point. When someone is dead, he can't speak for himself. It's not fair that someone is trying to put this on him."

"I don't know how far it will go," he said.

She sniffled. "I don't know how these things happen. But I know they happen in the low way of life. People wallow in the lowness, and they get it in their blood. Or maybe they have it in their blood and that's why they go there. For those of us who are there, it's hard to get out. I'm sorry to have lived a life where things like this seem like everyday events, and I hope to get out if I can." She paused. "But you didn't come here to hear about me."

Dunbar said, "It's all important."

She puffed out a breath. "Well, I think I said everything I had in mind at the moment."

I said, "I thank you for it, and I assure you again that we won't divulge any of this unless it seems necessary."

"That's up to you. I felt that I had to tell someone."

I thought she might say something about her

uncertainty about her own life, and her eyes seemed to exchange some intelligence with Dunbar, but she said no more.

"Good enough," I said. "It's getting cold out here, and we need to get moving. We'll see you women to the center of town, and then we have a long drive through the night."

# 11

WES GALVIN WAS WAITING UP WITH TYLER WHEN WE pulled into the ranch yard and stopped at the bunkhouse. I told the story of how we had been delayed at the lumberyard and then by the search for Ned Hacker.

The boss shook his head and opened and closed his big hands as he stood by the stove. "This doesn't make sense. I don't know why someone would want to do such a thing to either of those boys. They were as different as night and day. About all they had in common was that they worked here."

Tyler said, "They had some of the same habits when they went to town, and that's where they both went missing."

"We've looked into that," I said. "Or I should say, the information came to us. They both patronized the same woman, and she doesn't seem to have anything to do with what happened to them. To the contrary, she came to us and told us what she knew. Well, as Dunbar said, she didn't tell us everything she knew about everything, but she told us how she knew these two boys. If anything, Kent had more of a reason to do something to Ned than the other way around, but even that would have been improbable, and he died first, anyway. Ned was jealous of Kent, but it wasn't enough for him to do something that big, and the circumstance of his having Kent's watch on him just doesn't make any sense at all."

The boss said, "I didn't put any stock in it when you first told us. But what was he jealous of, the saloon girl you mentioned?"

"She's more of a street girl, as far as that goes, but no. The jealousy was based on another girl, which I would rather not discuss in any more detail."

The boss exchanged a glance with Tyler. "Oh. I think I might have heard something like that. Sorry. But I go to town so little, and I don't know much about those things."

"Neither did I, or at least some of them. But I became aware of them. I don't know how much they matter, but nothing else has turned up."

"Well, it's enough for one night," said the boss. "Let's put the wagon in the barn. I want to keep that lumber out of the weather so it won't warp any more than it has to before we can get it cut and nailed together." He spoke to Dunbar. "You brought the horse he was riding?"

"Yes. It still has his saddle on it."

"We'll do the same as we did with Kent's. Wait until we know what else to do with their things." The boss shook his head. "I'm not superstitious, and I don't believe there's been bad luck hangin' over this place since the little Hook boy was bit by a rattlesnake, but you have to wonder."

Tyler said, "Ned believed in bad luck. He said that fellow Deke had bad luck from sleeping in Kent's bed and using his saddle."

"He said the same thing to us," I said. "But both those boys got their bad medicine in town." As soon as I said it, I realized there were two kinds of bad medicine. One was the spiritual kind, and one was the kind that a person could buy from a druggist. But I left it at that. As the boss said, it was enough for one night.

---

THE STACK of firewood in the bunkhouse had gone down in my absence, and when I built it back up, I saw that I was going to have to go out and gather more. I stopped at the barn to look in. The men had measured, squared, and sawed lumber all through the morning. The dimensional pieces that came from the sawmill were close but not exact in length, so a pile of small scraps had begun to accumulate. It was not going to make much of a difference in how much firewood I had, so I went on.

As we made our way into the fall, I was having to go farther and farther to find deadfall. The cold wind blew at me sideways as I pushed the wheelbarrow along the right side of the fence to the horse pasture. Up ahead, something flapped in the wind, as if a burlap bag or a piece of deerskin had caught on a strand of wire. As the object did not stay still, I could not make it out. Closer, I saw legs hanging down and what looked like feathers fanning out. The sight was unusual, and I did not get a coherent idea out of it at first. Some years past, I had seen the body of a small deer hanging upside down with an ankle sticking up between two twisted strands of barbed wire. It appeared to have caught its leg while jumping over and then to have been unable to get loose. I had also seen where people would hang a coyote or a jackrabbit that way. But this object was not that large, and it was not upside down. It had feathers. I tried to imagine a grouse catching its leg that way, and again it did not make sense, for the legs were hanging down, and they were furry like rabbit legs.

The thing was moving, but I did not think it was alive. Not until I was almost upon it did I see that it was an owl, tan and grey, with claws at the ends of its legs. Its wings were caught on a single strand of wire, and it was well beyond any state of life. How long it had taken to die I did not know, as with the deer. But I thought I had to take it down and not leave it there to flap and decompose through the winter.

I had my gloves on, so I did not have to touch the dead thing with my bare hands, but both wings were wrapped tight in the wire. I retraced my route to a chokecherry bush, where I tore out a dead branch almost an inch thick. I broke it into a manageable length and used the stick to pry between a wing and the wire. The wing had wrapped a couple of times, so I had quite a bit of prying to do. At last I worked it free.

The second wing was much harder, even when I had the first one loose. The wire was imbedded so deep that I could not tell which way it should come out. I could turn the body over and over, but I could not dislodge it, and I could not slide it on the wire.

The body was light in weight, but it was not dry and stiff. A few drops of blood fell from it as I tried to work it loose. I thought the cold weather might have kept it from drying out sooner. But the wing was inflexible, and I felt that I was not having any effect.

Without my having done anything different, the wing came loose, and the bird fell from my grasp. For once, I had not cut myself when I was working around barbed wire. I used the stick to turn the owl over, and I saw the dark face and the short, fierce, curved beak. I broke the stick in half to carry the bird on it, in a kind of bier. After a little maneuvering, I had the body steady. At that point, I saw the undersides of its feet with the long, curved, slender claws. I wondered how many mice, rabbits, snakes, and even barnyard kittens this predator had taken before it came skimming along and hit the strand of steel wire at full force.

I carried the body down into the draw to a place where an old fox or badger den had an opening in the hillside. I pushed it in and left the two sticks to block some of the entry.

I thought the bird was a great horned owl, but it looked smaller in its ravaged state, and its feathers had flattened. I had no way of knowing if it was the one that had perched at the ranch a couple of times, but I did not see or hear another owl in the ranch yard through the rest of the fall and winter.

---

I HAD COOKED the last of the deer meat into a stew and had baked three tin plates of biscuits when the men came in for noon dinner. I was moving back and forth from the kitchen and saw that four men had trooped in. I had to take another look to see that the fourth man was Deputy Caryl.

He walked to the warming stove and held out the

palms of his hands. Tyler and Dunbar each set down a bucket of wood scraps.

"Just in time," I said.

The deputy moved his small chin and said, "Sometimes I have a knack for it."

Tyler threw in a few pieces of scrap lumber, and by the time the men had washed their hands, the pine was popping and throwing out sparks.

The men sat down to eat, and the deputy took care of his share. When the biscuits were gone and the men were done clacking their bowls, I said to the deputy, "I'm sorry I don't have any pie this time, but I cooked up some speckled puppy."

He drew his brows together. "What's that?"

"A chuck wagon delicacy. Boiled rice with raisins."

"Oh, I've had that before. It's good."

"I'll bring it out. I hope no one minds using the same bowl."

When the dessert was gone and the men were drinking coffee, the deputy pushed his chair back and hiked one foot onto his knee. In a relaxed style, not quite a drawl, he said, "I already asked the others about the deceased. I don't think I need to ask you all of the same questions. But the one I will repeat is whether you have any idea of why anyone would want to do something to him."

"He may have been annoying to some people, but not to that degree. The only specific motive I can think of would be to plant the watch on him, and that is a small motive."

"And of course, that's just a theory. We don't know it for a fact."

"Well, then, I think we covered all of that last night."

"You don't know where he went after you left him at one o'clock."

"No. I told you that."

"Thad Coulter said he saw him in the alley a little earlier. Why do you think that would be?"

"I don't know for a fact." I glanced at the others, and they were paying attention in such a way as to suggest that this line of questioning was new to them.

"You don't have any idea?"

"If I was pressed on it, I might have a theory."

"Well, we have time for it."

I felt that he was putting me on the spot in front of the others, and I did not like it. But I did not have the privilege of age with him, and a man had been killed. I said, "He may have been wondering where someone was."

"Your niece."

I flinched. "Yes. As you may know, she had been working in the mercantile store, and she had changed places of employment. She had gone to the café that is opening again."

"And he didn't know where she was?"

"I don't know what he did or did not know, but he did not seem to."

"These other men tell me that he seemed ill-humored around Kent Norland and took quite an interest in when and where he might be found."

"We touched upon some of that last night, but, yes, I noticed what you just mentioned."

"Do you think he might have been trying to find out any more about that—about who killed Kent Norland?"

I reviewed what I thought I had seen. "I don't know, again, and I don't want to speak of him in a slighting way, but he didn't seem to care very much, once they—or you—found the body."

The deputy nodded. "Maybe one other question. Can you tell me how to get to George Marven's place?"

"I don't think Ned Hacker knew him."

"No, but you do, and Miss Renfro does, so I'm looking into all my leads."

"None of this is a secret," I said, "as far as his being another relative, and where he lives. But I can tell you how to get there. You go southeast from here about ten miles. Look for a hill with a flat top—not what I'd call a butte, just a grassy hill. His place is just east of it. For that matter, he's straight south of town, if you want to go back that way after you've talked to him."

"I might."

When the deputy left, the men stayed a while longer as the last of the wood chips blazed and sent off the scent of pine.

Wes Galvin said, "That fellow has a lot of questions. Sometimes I think he doesn't care about the answer to half of them, and he likes to ask them in a peculiar order. What do you think, Tyler?"

"He likes to ask the same question in different ways."

I said, "He makes me feel guilty."

Dunbar waved his hand. "I think he knows you're not."

I laughed. "How do you know I'm not?"

"Same way you know I'm not. I've been with you all the time that both these young fellas have disappeared."

"What do you think of his questions?" asked

Galvin. "He says he wants facts, but he asks about opinions and theory."

Dunbar shrugged. "It's his way. He knows what he thinks of the answers he gets."

---

Wes Galvin licked the spoon that had been in the jam pot, and he set it on his plate. All the flapjacks were gone. I had thought I might have made too much batter, as I was still getting used to having a smaller number to cook for. But the cakes were gone, and the morning coffee was going as well.

"Here's my idea," said the boss. "We'll start framing the walls today. I want everything to be as square and precise as we can make it. Just like the cuts. We build these things in stages. As soon as you slip and say, 'Oh, that's good enough,' it grows. The next part is off or out of square, and so on."

Tyler and Dunbar nodded in agreement.

"So we build these walls. As I said before, they're going to be heavy, and the long ones even more so, but I think we can stand them up and put them in place. Rye can help with that part. Another hand would be better, but we can get by. Still, to keep these walls plumb and even to get them nailed together just right, we need at least four."

Dunbar said, "You can stand these walls up and brace 'em with a board and a stake every so often."

"I know. But even with that, this lumber's so thick and rough, and we have to drive the nails so hard, that it shakes. So two to hold, one to keep things plumb, and one to pound the nails." The boss looked around to make sure everyone was following him. "That's the walls. I've got it figured for three days to frame 'em together and stand 'em up. The last part won't take so long, but we need to do it in the best daylight and no hurry. That's when we need the fourth man. Rye."

He took a drink of coffee, and the others did as well.

"Now for the roof. We're going to do joists and rafters. The joists are the ones that run horizontal, from wall to wall. People call them rafters, but we won't because we want to keep things straight when we're talking. Rafters are the ones that go up on a slant and support the roof. Now, in order to put these things together, keep the ridge line straight, and not have any sway in the roof, everything has to be done right, up in the air. I'll be damned if I'm going to put in all this money and all this work and have a swayback roof for everyone to see."

He paused until we all nodded.

"Now to do this part, the way I have it figured, we need four men all day for at least two days. One man on each wall, and two up in the air. We can build these things on the ground in big triangles, or trusses, which I think is better than fitting everything together up there. Still, there's a lot of heavy nailing to be done up at the peak, to get those pieces spaced and joined just right, and we need two men up there. We need one man on each wall, to make sure the wall doesn't bow in or out and to make sure the joist doesn't move side to side, even when you have it toenailed in place. These things move, and I'm not going to turn my back on it just for the lack of having another man on the job. And if we want to eat, we can't have Rye out there all day each day."

As a general practice, the boss did not give such

long presentations, but I knew he had thought about this project at great length, and the threat of bad weather was always present as well. He went on.

"I don't know why things happen the way they do, and I don't want to dwell on myself when two good workers have died. And I don't want to dwell on why the sheriff's office takes so long to do so little. I feel bad for the loss of these two men. Things like this shouldn't happen, and it's bigger than my personal concerns. But I still have to look out for myself. I hired an extra man with this work in mind, and I lost one. I hired another, and he got banged up. Then I lost another. With all respect to them, it puts me in a bind, and I need another hand."

He seemed to have run out of steam after such a long speech, with its apology built in, and his hand had a slight shake as he took up his coffee cup again.

I said, "Do you think you want to go to town to look for another man?"

He shook his head. "I don't want to be gone that long at this point. And with what has happened, I don't want to send one man by himself."

"Do you have more lumber to pick up?"

"The freighters are supposed to deliver the next shipment straight to here. There's quite a bit, with all the boards for the outside, as well as the longer pieces for the joists and rafters."

"And the queen posts," said Tyler.

The boss gave him a questioning frown.

"Just being humorous for the moment. It was a term I heard once."

"That's all right," said the boss. "But back to the question. If any of you can think of someone we could hire for a while, that would help. Two of you could go into town on horseback, take an extra horse, and not take so long as you would with the wagon."

"I can think of one person," I said.

The boss had put his hands together and was staring at them. He perked up and said, "Who's that?"

"His name is Alan. He's the boy who works at the mercantile, does odd jobs, and runs errands."

"He's not some ten-year-old, is he?"

"No, he's about eighteen, I think. He might be willing to leave the job he has. But I don't know if he could drop everything in a minute. He would have to give notice to Fell, and as I recall, he also takes care of some lady's chickens. Lets them out in the morning and puts them up at night. He would have to find someone to do that."

The boss gave a light shake of the head. "The world is full of little things. But it reminds me. Once I have a feed shed, I'll want a cat to keep down the mice. So we can be on the lookout for one of those. Like I say, a small thing."

"When would you like someone to go?" I asked.

"When we have the walls up. I imagine you and Dunbar can go. If the other lumber arrives in the meanwhile, Tyler and I can start measuring and cutting for the joists and rafters. And queen posts."

---

The men framed the walls on the barn floor, with the plan of carrying them out when they were all ready. I heard the rat-tat-tat of the hammers through the morning.

A little before noon, I heard the creak of a wagon and the snuffle of horses outside the bunkhouse, so I went to the door and opened it. Instead of a freighter with a load of lumber, I saw two men in dark town clothes. One was Raymond Fell, wearing a long, black overcoat and a short-brimmed hat with a round crown. The other man was his clerk, Herman, wearing a black cap of dyed fur and a flecked, dark grey ulster. I wondered if they had left Alan to mind the store.

"How do you do?" I said.

Fell smiled without showing his teeth. "Very well. We brought out the merchandise that we spoke of the other day."

"Oh, yes. You can put the things in here, out of the way." The sound of hammers carried. "The men are building walls in the barn."

"Ah." Fell climbed down from the wagon and waited for Herman.

The clerk's movements were slow and stiff, and I did not know if it was from the bulk of the coat or from the long ride. When he moved to the back of the wagon, I saw that he was wearing overshoes with a regular pair of street shoes inside. The overshoes had thick soles, which I thought may have contributed to his stiffness.

The merchandise, as Fell had mentioned in the store, consisted of two kerosene lamps, a pair of heavy door hinges, a door latch, and a block and tackle—all things for the new shed. I did not see why they required separate delivery by two men, but I assumed that Fell wanted to stay on good terms with his customers. I imagined that he brought the clerk along in order for him to see the country, but the man did not seem used to the cold, even though the temperature was not that low for November.

They did not take long to store the items inside. I

invited them to stand by the stove, and I put in a few pieces of elm branches that I thought would blaze up. Fell took off his hat and coat, but Herman stayed bundled in his cap, overcoat, and pattens.

At last the man seemed to warm up. He took off his cap and coat and hung them next to Fell's. The two of them stood now with their backs to the stove and now with their fronts. Fell took out his cigarette case, opened it, offered a tailor-made to his clerk, and selected one for himself. He helped himself to a paper spill from my jar, lit their two cigarettes, and tossed the spill into the fire. Fell had been in the bunkhouse before, and he acted quite at home. He put one foot on the rail of the stove and spread his shoulders. Herman, on the other hand, stayed hunched together, and his beady eyes darted out.

I had been moving back and forth from the kitchen, and I could see they were in no hurry to leave. I said, "It's getting close to dinnertime, and I'm planning to fry up some pork to go along with some spuds I boiled. Nothing fancy, but you're welcome to eat with us. Keep the fire going for your trip back."

Fell blew his cigarette smoke up into the air. "That's very kind of you, Mr. Ryerson. I don't see how we could turn it down."

Herman forced a smile with his red lips.

In spite of his calling me "Mr. Ryerson," I thought I detected less of an ingratiating manner than before, and I imagined he no longer saw me as a benevolent uncle.

The workmen came in, and Fell introduced his employee to the boss and then Tyler. He turned his shoulder to Dunbar and waved in his direction as he spoke to Herman. "I believe you two have met."

When the meal was ready, Herman took the seat closest to the stove. Fell sat across from him, and as usual, he did not rest his glance on Dunbar or say a word to him. Herman, on the other hand, gazed at everybody and everything. He remained silent, and his face had little expression. In the lamplight, I saw that his complexion had a yellowish undertone, like jaundice, but the shadow of his close-shaved beard and the tinge of his lips drew a person's attention to those tones.

Knives and forks clacked on the crockery plates. Without looking up, Fell said, "Sorry to hear about your hired hand."

"It hits us hard," said the boss.

"I'm sure it does. I hope your building project is going well."

"We're moving along."

"Glad to hear it. And of course, if there's anything else we can provide, we'll be right there."

"I'm on the lookout for a cat. If I have sacks of grain, I'm liable to have mice."

"Oh, yes. Well, I'll keep it in mind."

When the meat and potatoes were gone, I brought out the pot with the dessert.

Fell spoke up in a cheerful tone. "What have we got here?"

"Stewed dried apples," I said, "with raisins for a sweetener."

"I'm sure it's good."

"It is," said the boss. "But they're like beans. They have that effect."

Fell paused. "Oh. I didn't know that."

Herman made a slow turn of the head. He had what seemed to be a controlled expression on his face, as if someone had asked him if he would like to hang a dog and he was deciding how to reply.

Tyler was sitting on Herman's right. His voice came up, as cheerful as Fell's had been. "How long have you been in town?"

"Not long," said Herman.

I wondered again if they had left Alan tending the store. Fell glanced to the side as he brushed at the sleeve of his jacket. He did not seem pressed by anything. I wondered if he would even care if we hired Alan away from him.

## 12

THE WALLS OF THE NEW BUILDING WERE STANDING LIKE bare ribs when Dunbar and I set out for town. I had brushed and saddled Partner, while Dunbar had rigged his blue roan. He led a sturdy brown horse that Tyler had fitted out with an extra ranch saddle.

"We can take it at a fast walk," said Dunbar. "No hurry. The weather's fair, and we're getting a good start."

I did not feel that he was trying to give orders. Rather, I felt that he was relieving me of any sense I might have that we should travel at a pace faster than I was comfortable with.

The pale sunlight that had gleamed on the new lumber was melting the frost on the grass and sagebrush, but not fast. The horses stepped out, and their energy carried on the air. At other times of the year, when I thought of the latter part of November, I pictured cold, windy weather with snowdrifts under grey skies, but as I thought of it now, I could remember other years when the temperate weather had lasted this long.

"I hope the good weather holds out," I said.

"So do I. I'm thinking of when it comes time to work on the roof. Frost on the lumber can send a fellow sliding right off. Bad way to fall."

"I've heard of it."

Dunbar spoke to the horse he was leading and returned to me. "I knew a fellow who took a fall that way. Landed on his feet. Broke 'em both."

"I've heard that on steep roofs, some workers tie themselves off."

"I know of a story like that, too, but it's in *Oliver Twist.* As I recall, the character is on a difficult roof and is trying to get away. He ties off, but the rope ends up around his neck, and he slips. He just murdered a girl, so he gets what he deserved. Like I said the other day, I should read that one again."

I wondered how much of a fund he had of stories in which people came to grief. "On another topic," I said, "I need to think about what to do if this kid can't go with us. The boss said to try to get someone. Problem is, there are only so many people in a small town. Then again, newcomers pass through, like Deke."

"Or Herman."

The man's cold face crossed my mind. "I can't quite picture him working on the roof."

"Just as well. I wouldn't want to turn my back on him."

---

Smoke was curling up out of stovepipes when we rode into Eminence. I stopped when we came to the corner where the bank stood on our right and the livery stable on our left.

I said, "I have to think of a plan for talking to this kid. I don't want to walk into the store and try to hire him away under Fell's nose. Vivian might be able to tell me something about his schedule. But before we go there, let's see about leaving this horse here at the livery stable. I feel conspicuous leading him down the main street."

I left the horse in a stall and said I would call for it later. Outside, I took my reins from Dunbar, and we rode toward the café.

We had ridden a little more than a block when Dunbar stopped his horse. My heart sank at the sight of two men walking out of the mercantile and turning left. I did not think they noticed us, but I did not mistake them. Fell and Herman were headed in the direction of the café. I did not want to cross paths with them, and if they were going into the café, I was afraid for the discomfort they would cause Vivian.

"I don't like the looks of that," I said.

"Neither do I," said Dunbar. "But it's broad daylight, so I imagine they're going there as customers. I doubt that they would do anything too forward, but if they start, I think Mrs. Deville will cut it short."

"That's assuring."

"Besides, it gives you the opportunity to talk to the young man."

"It does at that."

We waited until the two men crossed to the next block, with the buildings still on their left, and turned into the café. We angled across the main street, dismounted, tied up in front of the mercantile, and went in.

Alan met us in the center aisle. "Good morning, Mr. Ryerson. I can help you with your order. Mr. Fell has stepped out, but he can write you up as soon as he comes back."

I spoke in a low voice. "I'm not here to buy anything, Alan. Are you here by yourself?"

The boy widened his eyes and said, "Yes. Is there something wrong?"

"No. Or at least not that I know of. I came here to mention a job opportunity. I don't know how long it will last, and I don't know how willing you are to leave here."

Alan kept his voice low. "I would give anything to get out of here. But I'm afraid to do anything to make Mr. Fell angry." His eyes searched me. "What kind of work is it?"

"Building a shed. Like a small barn. The boss needs someone to work at the helper or laborer level."

The boy's eyes were still wide open. "I think I can do that. And even if it didn't last very long, it would get me out of here."

"Good. When do you think you could go?"

"I think I should work the rest of the day. Then I can tell him I have another job to go to. If I walk out in the middle of the day, I'm afraid he might lose his temper."

"All right," I said. "It's a little later than we were hoping, and I knew you would have to make some arrangements for the lady's chickens as well."

"Oh, yes. I almost forgot about that. I'll think of someone to take my place, but I should stay to do it this evening. And I'll have to talk to my ma. I can do that when I go home for dinner."

"Very well," I said. "Let's set a time and place." I had understood that his mother kept a small and cluttered house and did not let people come in. "How about the café, at seven or a little after? We can ride to the ranch after that. You can ride a horse that far, can't you?"

"Oh, yes. I think so."

"All set, then. We'll get out of here before someone comes back."

"Thanks, Mr. Ryerson. If anything comes up, I'll let them know at the café."

Dunbar and I walked out into the street. I did not want to seem as if I was in a hurry, but I did not loiter. I kept myself from looking down the street toward the café as I untied Partner's reins and began to walk him to the west. Dunbar fell in alongside.

"We have plenty of time," I said. "What do you think about dropping in to see how our old friend Deke is doing?"

"As good as anything else," he said.

We found Deke McGinley in the front room of the hotel. He was sitting in front of the coal-burning stove with a newspaper on the table beside him. He was wearing a grey flannel shirt, and his face had the same pale color as when we first met him.

"Well, hello, boys," he said, standing up. "I didn't know if I'd see you again."

I shook his hand and said, "I didn't know if you had left town."

"To tell you the truth, I can't afford to. What I need is to be able to find a little bit of work to pay my bill here and to give me some travel money." He shook hands with Dunbar.

"Do you think you can work?" I asked.

His eyebrows went up. "Depends on what kind."

"The boss still needs to get his shed built. All the cement and rock work is done, as you might recall, and so is the heavier part of putting up the walls. Right now he needs someone to hold one end of a roof truss while they get the pieces plumbed and lined up. After that, there'll be a lot of boards to nail."

"I'd sure like to give it a try. It's hell bein' broke."

I felt sympathy for him, and even though I hadn't done anything, I felt guilty on behalf of the ranch. I said, "I might be taking too much upon myself, but let's say there's a possibility, at least. I've already talked to one person, a kid, and if he can't go, I can call on you. I won't know for sure until about seven this evening."

Deke's face relaxed in his uneven smile. "I'm not doin' anything else."

"Do you think you can ride a horse?" I asked. "To get to the ranch."

"I think I can do that much. With one of you on each side, I shouldn't have much to worry about a horse takin' off or actin' up."

"I'll let you know, then, one way or the other. At about seven."

"That's good of you, Rye. Thanks. And thanks to you, Dunbar, for comin' by to see an old man."

Dunbar laughed. "I'd miss my bet if you're any older than I am."

"I just feel that way. But I hope to get over it."

Outside, I peered down the empty street. I said to Dunbar, "Judging from the way Alan spoke and from the time of day, I would bet that the Barber of Seville and his employer went for no more than a cup of coffee and to take a look at things."

"With an emphasis on the latter. That fellow Herman is not very subtle."

"Let's go around the long way and come in from the east. It will give them more time to be gone, and we won't have to ride past the store."

My hunch proved out all right. The café was open but empty of customers. I noticed on the way in that the letters on the window had been repainted in a similar light green.

Mrs. Deville gave Dunbar a steely expression and said, "You might guess who came in here not long ago."

"The Merchant of Venice and the Barber of Seville. We saw them from down the street."

"I hadn't thought of that sallow one as a barber. More like a butcher, perhaps."

"It's a nickname someone else came up with. They didn't do any harm, did they?"

"No, but they looked everything over. Vivian went to the kitchen to stay with Madeline." Mrs. Deville gave me a smile. "And what brings you lads to the village today?"

"The boss would like another hand for the building project. They've got the walls up, but to put together the roof structure, he'd like at least one more hand. I've talked to Alan, and if he can't go, we might take along a fellow who worked a couple of days last week."

"The one I told you about the other day," said Dunbar. "The one who had a horse go over on him."

"Oh, yes." After a second, she added, "I hope he does all right."

I looked around for a clock and found one on a shelf behind the counter. I said to Dunbar, "It's almost noon, and we have time on our hands. Shall we try the food here?"

"On one condition. That I be the host. You can have your turn in the next place we go to."

I imagined he meant the Double Eagle, and I was not afraid that he would keep me in there all afternoon. "All right," I said.

---

THE OUTSIDE TEMPERATURE had not climbed much since we left the ranch at about nine, and a light breeze was stirring. I was not fond of sitting in a saloon through the afternoon, and I was not one to sit in front of a store and shell peanuts, but I did not have any other tasks or errands. If I had been at the ranch, I might have done a little more work on my walking stick, if there wasn't a building to be worked on.

I said to Dunbar, "I don't like being idle like this when there's work to be done at home and we have to wait a few hours until we can leave. I don't care to spend all that time in the Double Eagle."

"Neither do I," he said. "What would you think of taking a ride to the Blue Diamond?"

"That's an idea. Do you think we'll find out something there?"

"It's worth a try."

I glanced at the sky. "Might as well."

---

A LITTLE MORE THAN an hour's ride took us to the road ranch. I had not been inside, or around back, but I knew the building on sight. It was a one-story frame structure with a front about fifty feet long. The building went back for about thirty feet, and from there, a couple of small additions had been built on. Also visible from the road were a couple of outbuildings.

The front did not have a veranda or overhang, just a door to the right of center and a curtained window on either side. An empty hitching rail suggested that business had not picked up for the day.

We dismounted, tied our horses, and knocked on the door. After a long minute, footsteps sounded on a wood floor inside. An interior door opened and closed, and the latch on the front door clicked. The door swung inward to show us the round-shouldered man with a heavy brow and dark shadows under his eyes. His mouth hung open. He was wearing his bowler hat, an ivory-colored shirt with brown armbands, and a brocade vest of silver and dark brown. He was thick in the chest and waist, with a long torso. He wore dark grey striped pants, and a black belt and holster carried a small pistol on his right hip. He rested his hand on his waist above the pistol and swept a glance over the two of us.

"What'll it be?"

Dunbar said, "We were in the neighborhood, so we thought we'd drop in."

"You and our uncle?"

"Do you have an age restriction?"

"No. Just height. No one comes in here unless his nose comes above this doorknob." He looked us over to see that neither of us was carrying a sidearm, and he stepped aside to let us into the entryway.

I did not like being that close to him, but he opened the interior door and let us into the front room or what I would call the parlor.

A brown, corduroy-covered sofa sat against the back wall. To its left as I faced it, a red velvet curtain covered what I assumed was a passage to other rooms. On the right end of the sofa, at a right angle to it, sat a plush armchair of a deep maroon color. Three wooden chairs with dark red velvet cushions sat opposite the sofa at a six-foot distance. At the left end of the room, in dimmer light, a bar of polished wood faced the sitting area.

The doorman crossed in front of us and pulled on the black handle of a chain that hung next to the drape. I heard a bell ping farther in. Without looking at us, the doorman lumbered to the northwest corner of the room and stood by the bar.

The curtain moved, and a brown-haired female came out. She had blue eyes, freckles, and a full, short-waisted figure. She stepped aside and was joined by a woman with a slender build and sandy-colored hair.

The woman with brown hair smiled and said, "Hello, boys. What are you up to?"

Dunbar said, "Thought we'd drop in and see who was here."

The woman smiled again and said, "We're glad you did. I'm Maisie, and this is Peg."

We took off our hats.

Maisie said, "What are your names? Don't be shy."

Dunbar waited for me to speak.

I did not expect to do anything with these girls, but

my heartbeat had picked up nevertheless. I said, "Rye."

Maisie turned to Dunbar, with a movement of her bosom. "And yours?"

"Scotch."

"Scotch and Rye. Oh, how cute! We're going to have a party."

Peg moved close to me and put her hand on my arm. "What would you like to do first? Have a drink and relax a little?"

I realized that if we were not going to engage their favors, we were going to have to have a drink. "I suppose so," I said.

The doorman moved behind the bar, lit a lamp, and became the barman. As the four of us approached, he said, "What'll it be?"

"Bourbon," said Dunbar.

Maisie laughed and put her hand on his arm. "We'll get to the rest of your vocabulary if it takes all day."

"And you?" said the bartender.

I said, "Beer if you have it."

"In a glass."

"Just the way I like it."

He poured Dunbar a shot glass of whiskey, and he poured me a small glass of beer. I laid a silver dollar on the bar.

"Pay as you go," he said. "Some guys forget, and some run out of money."

I had heard the word "guy" before, and I was not surprised to hear it come from him.

Maisie said, "This is Cage. He looks out for everything. Cage, maybe you already know these gentlemen."

His shadowed eyes passed over us. "I know who they are. They're pals of the sniveler who was found dead and lost his watch."

Dunbar raised his eyebrows in an innocent expression. "I knew him for just a few days. Why do you call him a sniveler?"

"I knew him at Fetterman. Always came mooning around."

"Poor boy," said Maisie. "I knew him, too. He came out here."

My teeth clenched.

"Sniveler," said the bartender.

Peg touched my arm. "Don't worry about these other people." She had soft, brown eyes, and in another time and place, I might have found her more appealing.

"It's nothing," I said.

"Let's just have a good time," said Maisie.

The red curtain moved, and a woman in a bright green dress walked through. She had blond hair and a full figure, and she approached us with a seductive sway. I noticed her dark blue eyes and painted red lips, but the exposed cream-colored upper level of her bosom made me look away.

Her voice was lively and had command. "And how are you two gentlemen today? You've met my girls, I see. I don't think you've been here before, so I want to welcome you and tell you what's available." She waved her hand. "My girls are clean, and they're as good as any you'll find in a hundred miles. They may have already told you, but you can go to the room with either of them for a dollar." She ran her hand from the side of her bosom down to her hip. "If you want to go for the best, it's five dollars."

I still could not look full on her.

"What's your name?" asked Dunbar.

"Florence," said the woman. "People know my name, Florence Mallow, and my place has a good reputation. Are you from around here?"

"I haven't been here long."

"Well, don't be shy."

She relaxed in her pose, and I ventured a glance at her. Her dark blue eyes were shining, and her red lips were smiling. Then in the small cream-colored expanse, I saw something that made time stand still.

Hanging on a small gold chain, almost touching her cleavage, lay a pendant with a shiny green emerald and a sparkling diamond above it.

My mouth was dry, and my heart was in my throat.

"Are you deciding?" said the madam.

I realized she was talking to me. I found my breath and my voice as I swallowed, cleared my throat, and met her eyes. "Not today," I said.

She brandished herself at Dunbar. "And you?"

He smiled. "Also not today. Although I wouldn't dispute a word you have said."

I had regained my senses, and I knew that I could hang onto them if I did not let myself look at the pendant. I could steal a glance to be sure of it, but I could not let my eyes rest on it.

"You want to try them all," said the madam. "Sooner or later, in one place or another, you'll see them all—black and red and brown and yellow and white, tall and short, round and thin, sweet and sour. You get what you pay for, and in the best places, the price and the value go together." She patted Dunbar on the upper arm. "Do you believe me?"

He arched an eyebrow and said, "I heard once, or

read, that the price of something is equivalent to the amount of your life that you exchange for it."

"That could be," said the woman. "Nothing is free."

Dunbar continued. "Like I said, I learned that idea and remembered it. So it's not original to me. I sort of adopted it."

The woman tossed her head. "No harm in that. Your deepest thinkers get hungry and thirsty." She touched his arm. "You boys enjoy yourselves." With her swaying motion, she left us and passed through the red curtain.

I took a drink from my beer. It was not cold, but it helped my dry throat.

"So what do you think?" said Peg. This time she ran the back of her finger down the front of my coat. She stopped above my waist.

I said, "I think you're a charming girl, but my sap's not rising today." I found a silver dollar in my pocket, drew it out, and gave it to her. "A small token."

"Thank you."

Dunbar handed a dollar to Maisie. "We've enjoyed your company today, girls. We can't stay long. We'll look forward to the next time."

"When your sap's rising," said Maisie.

"You never know."

We finished our drinks, said goodbye, and left.

On the trail toward town, I said to Dunbar, "Not such a bad place, once you get past the doorman."

"I suppose they need someone like him. At least in that position."

"The madam is civil enough. Not lewd, like some I've known."

Dunbar clucked to his horse. "Say what you will,

it's a straightforward business that she runs. So it seems. She may not be the fabled harlot with a heart of gold, but she struck me as honest."

"Not to mention attractive."

"Oh, yes. She has her charms."

"Did you notice the pendant she was wearing?"

"Yes, I did. It's a kind of jewelry I've seen before, but I think it's the first time I've seen it in that arrangement. Any reason?"

"Not at the moment. Or, as I told her when I caught my breath, not today."

---

WE RETURNED to town by way of the east side as the sun was beginning to drop in the southwest. The yellow light was turning to orange, and the scattered clouds were dark in the center. I figured we had more than two hours to wait, and I hoped not to pose an inconvenience to Mrs. Deville.

She surprised me, however, by handing me a folded piece of common writing paper. "Alan left this for you earlier in the afternoon," she said.

I broke the thin wafer of wax and read the note.

*DEAR MR. RYERSON:*

*I will not be able to go with you this evening. It will take me until tomorrow to have things arranged. I can walk to the ranch. I know where it is, and I have walked that far before.*

*Alan*

I HANDED the note to Dunbar. When he had read it, I said, "I wish I had known this earlier. But we can still get started a couple of hours sooner than I thought. Let me write him a note at the bottom here. I'll tell him to come on out. If the boss wants to send someone with a horse, he can, but I won't decide that for him."

I wrote my note, and Mrs. Deville lent me a candle to seal the paper. "Hardly necessary to seal it," I said, "but the boy has a sense of what's proper, and I think it's courtesy to reply in kind."

"I'll hold it for him." She raised her eyes to Dunbar, who stood near the table where she and I sat. "Before you go, I think Madeline would like to speak with you again."

He glanced at the kitchen. "I imagine that would include the two of us."

We rose and walked to the kitchen, where Madeline and Vivian were finishing what seemed to be a cordial conversation. Vivian smiled at me and passed into the dining area.

Dunbar gave Madeline a perfunctory smile. "Mrs. Deville says you might like to talk."

Madeline's face had a downcast expression. "I'm sorry to keep adding things on, but I don't always know how much to say. I'm afraid to talk about some things, and then I'm afraid something will happen and I'll never get to."

"I wish I could assure you that—"

"I know you can't. And I don't know if I'd do more harm than good by spilling my guts, and I still don't know how much I want to say."

"Well, whatever you want to say, we'll listen." He waved his hand at me. "If something happens to one of us, it's still safe with the other."

She turned her green eyes to me, and I felt that she trusted me even as she worried. "I think outside is better, again," she said.

The shadows of evening were beginning to stretch, but I had the comfort of being able to see that no one was near.

Her voice sounded husky as she began. "It seems like all I talk about is the men who have paid me, but there's one more I think I should tell you about while I still can. I don't like to say names, but he is a store owner. When he came in here earlier today with his clerk, I felt such a fear run through me that I knew I had to tell you."

She paused, and we both nodded for her to go on.

"He is the worst. I know that you are both gentlemen, and I wouldn't say this if I didn't think you know how to handle the truth."

As before, I felt that she had thought out what she wanted to say. I nodded again and braced myself.

"He is the worst," she said again. "When he is on me, I feel like I am doing it with the devil, and when he is done, it's as if I have the devil in me. Because he says in my ear before he gets off of me, 'I am in you now. I want you to know and remember that I am in you. It's my way of making you mine.' I tell you, I've done it with him only a couple of times, but it gives me a terrible feeling, and it's one of the reasons I'm trying to get away from all of that."

I felt a strange sense of unreality as well as repugnance as she was telling us this, but I knew she had an urgent feeling to confess to someone, and she had settled on us. So I tried to push aside the ugliness and to focus on the purpose.

Dunbar said, "You know we'll help if we can."

"Hearing me is a help."

"We're glad we were able to."

"I have a little more, but I don't know how important it is."

"Go ahead."

"I think I should have said this in an earlier conversation. I was going to say it first today, but I blurted out the other part. But it doesn't matter. What I want to say is I think he despised Kent. I think he found out that Kent went with me, and then he wanted to cover him by being with me himself. 'Cover' is the only word I can think of to describe it. Kind of like rub him out. Then he wanted to use what he knew about Kent as some kind of leverage or control. Like Ned did or said he was going to do. I think he wanted to threaten to tell someone about it."

"What other questions did he ask you about . . . Kent?" Dunbar seemed reluctant to name names as well, as she had been.

"He wanted to know if Kent ever said anything about him. I said no, because he didn't, although I think they were both at Fetterman at the same time."

"Did you ever know him from before?"

"Him?"

"The merchant."

"No. I didn't know either of them, for that matter."

"Where did you work before you came here?"

"Cheyenne. But you know, a girl can stay in one place for only so long, and then she has to move. It's just the way things are."

"I see. Going back to this leverage, then—why would he want leverage over the younger man?"

"Well . . . I think more than one person could tell

that he was stuck on the same girl. I don't think I'm saying anything new. But that was it, and then, when he didn't have any more competition, he had to give up on it. Still, I don't have good feelings for him or for the man he has working for him."

Dunbar said, "We appreciate your willingness to tell us these things."

"Like I said, some of it may not be new, and I don't want anyone to take it personal. I may have said more than I intended, but as for the rest, I'm glad I had the chance. When they came in today, I thought I had to."

The shadows had grown darker in the short time we had been outside, and the temperature was going down. She had not worn her coat, and she was holding her arms across her front.

"Anything else?" I asked.

She shook her head. "I feel worn out from saying as much as I did."

## 13

Stacks of lumber reflected the moonlight when Dunbar and I rode into the ranch yard with Deke McGinley between us. The boss showed surprise at seeing our recruit, and he welcomed him back. When I explained the situation with Alan, the boss said he might send someone if the crew reached a good stopping point the next afternoon, but he felt he was trying to beat the weather at the moment.

Although night had fallen and I had a sense that it was late, the bunkhouse clock showed a few minutes short of seven. Dunbar and Tyler put the horses away while Deke established himself in the bunkhouse again and I built a fire in the cookstove. Before long, I had meat and potatoes frying in the skillets.

In the conversation after supper, the boss was brimming with enthusiasm. He said the lumber had arrived in the afternoon and the count was good. If they didn't waste any and didn't have to toss out much warped or split wood, everything should work out.

He said they would begin building trusses the next

morning. Deke was showing interest and asked how he had them planned.

"With roof boards, I have them on two-foot centers."

"And how long is the building?"

"Twenty-four feet."

"Twelve of them, then."

"Thirteen," said the boss. "You need one on each end."

Deke's face did not show that he understood.

"It's like a loaf of bread," said Dunbar. He made a motion with his hand as if he was running his thumb and middle finger along the sides of a loaf on the table between them. "If you want to cut a loaf of bread into twelve pieces, you cut it eleven times. Then, like the boss says, you need one on each end."

"Thirteen," said the boss.

"Or eleven and two," said Dunbar. "In case anyone is superstitious. The two end ones will be a little different, anyway. We'll put in a couple of extra vertical pieces for bracing and to have more to nail to." He smiled at Tyler. "Like queen posts."

Deke spoke in his smooth voice. "Seems to me if you have two extra pieces, you should have fourteen."

"You'll see it tomorrow," said the boss. "It's something you get used to when you lay out walls or anything like that. One on each end, but only one is the extra, as you say."

Deke shook his head. "I'm not stupid. I just can't picture it. Too many of them to see and count in my mind."

"Think of it this way," said Dunbar. "If you want to cut a stick or a rope in three equal pieces, you cut it twice."

"That's right." Deke smiled. "I learned that when I was a kid. I might have ruined a rope, but I learned it."

"So there is always one less cut than the number of pieces, and in this case, the pieces of bread are the empty spaces between the trusses."

"Oh, hell. And the rafters are the cuts. We were calling them the pieces. That's where we get the eleven and then the two. Now I'll be able to sleep."

---

WITH THE LUMBER stacked in the yard, the men did all the sawing outdoors as well as the hammering. I went out to watch the industry. The boss and Dunbar laid out the first truss on the ground, as even and level as they could, and nailed it together with small pieces of one-by-four. After that, they used the first one as a template or pattern, building a new one on top of it and then putting the new one on a stack when it was finished.

The boss was happy to share what he knew. "Don't build one off of another, all the way along. Always go back to the first one. Otherwise, your last one and your first one are too far apart in measurement. Then, when you move 'em to the stack and put them on the building after that, don't turn one around. Keep 'em all faced the same way they came off the template. I learned all of this the hard way. I even learned how to figure the number of trusses the hard way. Had to build one in place, up in the air."

I nodded. I could tell that he had already told the workers all of this and did not mind them hearing it again.

The building of the trusses was slow work, with all

the cuts to be made, including on the small pieces that were used to splice the corners and the upright for the center. Each large triangle consisted of two smaller, back-to-back triangles—or, as Dunbar pointed out, three triangles in all, with more on the end trusses.

"Geometry and arithmetic. A kind of poetry in itself."

Optimism and good humor floated in the air. Deke McGinley was wearing the cloth cap and drab shirt he had worn to mix the cement. If I looked at him in a certain way, I could imagine him being a convict, but he had a smile on his face as he carried pieces of lumber and held them to be cut.

At any stray moment, thoughts from the outer world revisited me. Images from the conversation with Madeline Osborn fluttered down like crows on a carcass. And the shine of a diamond and an emerald on the background of a woman's skin carried across the miles like a homing bird on the wing.

In the latter part of the morning, I cut up carrots and onions and potatoes as well as chunks of meat. I cooked a beef stew that I hoped would do for both meals. We had been eating our own beef again, and I felt that I was cooking for a larger crew in a land of plenty.

In the afternoon, when I had finished washing the noon dishes, I built up the fire in the cookstove again and baked an apple pie. Most of the time, it seemed as if the ranch was a peaceful place far from the crowd, but then a thought would come winging in through the walls.

In the late afternoon, as I was listening to the music of the hammers and saws and was watching the stack of trusses grow, Alan came trudging in from the rangeland. He had a knapsack on his back and a bedroll slung on his shoulder. He wore a denim jacket, and his wavy, light brown hair stuck out beneath a dark blue cap of wide-wale corduroy. He leaned forward with the weight of his belongings, but his grey eyes had an open expression, and he gave a light smile as he stopped in front of me.

"No trouble getting here?" I asked.

"Not at all."

"Well, here's the boss. As you can see, they're humming along with the work."

I gazed at the open country the boy had walked across. At a time when Wes Galvin was cautious about sending a rider alone and when people in town were worried about walking after dark, he had walked the whole distance alone. Whether he had given it a thought, I did not know, but I appreciated his pluck.

The boss shook his hand and told him to put his things in the bunkhouse, so I showed him the way.

"No complications in town?" I asked.

"Not much. My ma didn't want me to go, but I told her it wouldn't be for all that long."

"She wasn't upset that you quit your other job?"

"I told her it wasn't any good since Vivian left. And it wasn't. Mr. Fell never treated me well to begin with, and Herman was worse. He reminded me of someone in a story who cut out people's livers."

"And you found someone to take care of the lady's chickens?"

"Yes. Madeline said she would do it."

"That's good. But doesn't she work later at the café?"

"I think she can get away. It doesn't take but a few minutes."

"I see. Well, here are the bunks. This one was Ned Hacker's. We haven't known what to do with his belongings yet, and some of Kent's things are beneath it. That last bunk might be better. It's empty."

The tenseness around his eyes faded. "That's good enough for me. Who's the stranger out there working with the others?"

"Oh, that's a fellow named Deke. He worked here for a couple of days and had an accident with a horse. He was in town for a while, and he just came back to work."

"I think I heard of him."

"The boss is glad to have the help. I think the work should go pretty smooth now."

---

I HAD COUNTED plates and places more than once, so I knew things would come out even when I cut the pie after supper. I put each piece on a plate and sent it down the table.

Deke was sitting across from Alan. He reminded me again of a Southern preacher when he said, "Tell me this, young man. Why is it that if you cut a loaf of bread into six pieces, you cut it five times, but if you cut a pie into six pieces, you have to cut it six times?"

Alan frowned. "I would guess it's because they're different shapes."

"All right. And let's say you had a shed that was twelve feet long, and you wanted to put a set of rafters every two feet. How many sets would you need?"

"Six. No, seven."

"So you have five, six, or seven. Why is that?"

"I don't know. Let me see. With the bread and the

pie, you're just cutting on the inside, so you have five lines and six. With the rafters, you're going on the outside, so you have seven."

"That's right," said Dunbar. "And with the pie, the circumference is the seventh line."

Alan's face brightened. "Like I said, different shapes."

Deke said, "That puts it all together. When you call them lines, it all makes sense. When we talked about this last night, we talked about the rafters as pieces and then the spaces between as pieces, like slices of bread. Then I saw the rafters as lines. It's clear as day if you look at the lines the boss drew on the tops of the walls where those rafters are goin' to go."

Dunbar paused with his fork by his piece of pie. "I sure didn't try to confuse anyone. I like to keep things sorted out whenever I can."

Still in his smooth voice, Deke said, "I can see it all now. You explained it at last, but the ideas were up in the air for a while. You're kind of a philosophical type."

Dunbar smiled. "If I am, it's what gets me in trouble. I'm better when I focus on things."

Deke waved. "That's all right. I'm not as dumb as I look." He wore his uneven smile. "Sometimes I think I got my head rattled when that horse fell on me. But the more I look at you, the more I think I've seen you before."

Dunbar glanced at me. "It might be from that evening you sang a song in the Double Eagle. Rye and I were part of the audience."

"By golly, that's it. When you're in front of a crowd, you don't always remember the individual faces. But you see 'em."

"You sing songs?" said Tyler.

"Just one. I made it up myself. I don't sing anyone else's songs, not for other people, and I don't play a piano or a guitar or anything. I'm just a one-song fella, but I'm workin' on another when I have time to myself."

Tyler said, "Why don't you sing it for us now?"

"I don't want to ruin your dessert."

The boss said, "We'll eat our pie, and then you can sing."

"I might be too nervous."

"We don't have any whiskey to calm you down."

"Oh, I don't want any of that. I had enough of it before."

"Then let's have our pie, and if you can hold yourself together, we can hear your song. If you can sing in the barroom, you can sing here."

When the last crumbs of pie were gone, Tyler and the boss coaxed Deke a little more. He put on his hat, took his stance in front of the stove, and delivered the song about the rustlers just as he had done in the saloon.

We all applauded, and the boss said, "That was good. Very good."

"It's not much, but it's what I can do."

"It's something the rest of us can't do," said Dunbar. "And you've got an ear for it. I think you could learn to play."

"I don't know. But I thank you-all for the kind words. Maybe I can go on to learn to do more."

A thoughtful expression passed over his face, and it occurred to me that for a moment, he might have thought he had seen Dunbar at Deer Lodge. Something told me that Dunbar had not been there but

Deke might well have. As for myself, I was used to being unnoticed by people who, unlike Cage Whitman, had no reason to remember me.

---

DEKE'S HAT and sheepskin coat lay on the foot of the bed when he went out to work with the others the next morning. Alan fit in with the crew right away, fetching nails and picking up wood scraps. When the time came to begin setting the trusses in place, the boss put Tyler on one wall, Alan on the other, and himself and Dunbar in the middle to do the high work.

Deke was the extra hand now. The boss fashioned him a two-by-two stick about eight feet long with a short tray across the top. The tray consisted of two pieces of one-by-four joined lengthwise at a right angle and set into the tip of the stick. It resembled a device called a hod, which a hod carrier used, except that the trough had open ends. Deke used it to help hold the truss upright and to hand up nails or anything that fell, such as a pencil, a length of string, or a hammer.

The first truss took almost an hour to be put into place, nailed, plumbed, and braced. The boss wanted the first one perfect, so that he would not have an error to be passed down the line and to grow as it went. Dunbar showed patience and dedication to the same degree of accuracy.

After the first truss, each one took about twenty minutes. The boss made sure they all faced the same way they had gone onto and come off the stack, and he took care to plumb each one and to cut and nail an exact spacer to connect it to the previous truss. He also used a string line to keep the ridge straight. I could see where a half-inch error could be committed anywhere by workers with good intentions but not the most demanding standards.

By late afternoon, the crew had the last truss in place, nailed, and braced like its partner on the other end. The number of trusses had not changed since they all went on the stack, but each worker counted them as I did, now that they were in place. Thirteen.

By the time the workmen picked up their tools and stacked the ladders on the sawhorses, the sun was beginning to go down. A clear but pale blue sky made a pretty contrast with clouds that changed from yellow to light orange to a pink-orange that reminded me of the color of the flesh of some fish. The underside of one bank of clouds had a mottled texture like the small feathers on the chest of a grouse. The sky changed every minute, and the dappled shadows on the clouds darkened as the sun went down. Closer in, the leafless branches of an elm tree showed in clear outline, and the hollow frame of the new building looked like a whole and perfect skeleton.

A good mood prevailed in the bunkhouse but nothing in the nature of celebration, as the next phase of work was waiting for the morning. After supper, Alan washed dishes. Tyler was braiding three strands of jute, for practice, and Dunbar was sewing up a hole in the toe of a grey wool sock. The boss was working at figures in his notebook, and Deke was lying on his bunk, staring at the ceiling with his hands behind his head.

Before going to bed, I went out to look at the night sky, as I often did when the weather was not too cold. The moon was a couple of days short of a full moon, and it had risen to the high point of the night. The scattered clouds were lying lower. In the moonlight, I could see the barn at its distance of forty yards as well as the frame outline of the new building.

I went to my bunk in my little area off from the kitchen, and I heard the others go to bed in the main area as usual. I went to sleep, thinking about what it would be like to work on the trains and to travel across vast landscapes in the moonlight.

I was jolted awake by a gunshot outside, not far from the wall where I slept. I heard something like a groan, then a mixture of voices and movement as the men in the next room sprang out of bed and went for their hats and boots and guns. I had pulled on my own boots and was hunching into my overcoat when I heard another shot. I grabbed my hat and hurried through the kitchen and main area and out into the night.

The moon had moved to the west and sunk a little, but visibility was still good. I recognized the figure of Dunbar in his hat, coat, long underwear, and boots. He was walking toward the bunkhouse while Tyler, dressed the same, stood waiting. Alan appeared at my side as the door of the ranch house opened and Wes Galvin stepped outside with a shining lantern.

"What's going on?" he called out.

Dunbar answered. "Someone fired a shot in back. I jumped and ran out, and I followed someone running toward the barn. I got off one shot, and then I lost him."

By now, the five of us had moved to form a group. The boss held up his lantern and said, "Is everyone here? Who's missing?"

Tyler said, "Deke."

With the boss lighting the way, we walked to the

end of the bunkhouse and followed it toward the back. Halfway to the outhouse, a form lay on the ground.

"Deke?" called the boss. "Is that you?"

The form moved, shifted onto one side, and sat up. The lamplight showed Deke McGinley in his sheepskin coat. His hat lay on the ground a few feet away.

"What happened?" asked the boss.

Deke moved his head. "I think someone shot at me. I came out to go to the outhouse, and out of nowhere I felt a *whoof* go through my coat and pull on my arm, and I heard a shot along with it. I didn't know if I'd been hit, but I went down so he wouldn't shoot me again."

I handed him his hat.

"Thanks." He put it on and pushed himself to his feet. Like the others, he was wearing boots, a hat, a coat, and long underwear. "I don't know if I've been hit. It doesn't feel like it."

The boss held the lantern while Dunbar and Tyler looked the man over. They found a small hole in the side of his coat and another in his sleeve, but they did not find any blood or wounds.

"I think I'm just damn lucky," Deke said.

"I don't know why someone would do something like that," said the boss. "Let's all go inside and not stand around out here like geese in the moonlight. I'll get dressed and meet you."

Inside, I lit a lamp and built up a fire, then put on the rest of my clothes and joined the others. Deke was shivering. He had gotten dressed and put on his coat again, but he had not gotten over the shock.

"This is strange as hell," said the boss.

"I'm just lucky," said Deke.

Dunbar said, "I don't know how lucky anyone is to be shot at from behind, but I'm glad you weren't hit."

Color had risen in the boss's face. "Why would someone shoot at him, though?"

"I can't say for sure," said Dunbar, "but I have a hunch. I think someone thought he was shooting at me, but his shot was off center, and Deke's a little thinner than I am."

The others looked at Dunbar and at Deke.

"We don't look alike from the front, but from the back, in the moonlight, it's feasible."

"That's true," I said. "I noticed it once myself. Deke's sheepskin doesn't look all that different from Dunbar's canvas coat if the light isn't good, and it makes him look bigger, or wider."

The boss turned to Dunbar. "Then why would someone want to shoot at you?"

"If I knew who it was, I might have a better idea."

"But you got a shot at him."

"I did. But I don't know if I hit him."

"Well, let's go look and see. We're all dressed. Deke, do you want to stay here?"

Deke exerted a shiver and stopped. "I'm gettin' over it. I want to see right along with the rest of you."

I lit a second outdoor lantern, and the six of us went out. The boss and I showed the way, and Dunbar led in the middle. A little more than halfway to the barn, he stopped.

"Show the light closer. That looks like a drop of blood. Let's go this way."

A few steps later, he stopped again. "That looks like another one."

We went on that way, past the barn and out onto the road that led to town. Five yards to the left of the road, a dark form lay in the moonlight. The boss and I hurried forward, holding up our lanterns.

We stopped at the man's body. I had a pretty good idea of who it was, although he had a black knitted cap pulled down over his forehead and ears. He was wearing a dark coat of a stitched rag-like cloth, but the corner was folded back and revealed a khaki shirt, a leather vest, and a knife scabbard with a thong at the tip.

"Does anyone know him?" asked the boss.

I said, "He goes by the name of Critter. He's a troublemaker who has been hanging around town."

The boss faced Dunbar. "What does he have against you?"

"I ran into him a couple of times when I was asked to tell him to leave a woman alone."

"And he walked all the way out here to take a shot at you for that?"

"I don't think he walked. I think I heard a horse running away. And as for why, he may have had someone else to nudge him."

"And who would that be?"

"I need to study it a little more before I say any names."

Alan had moved forward to see the body. "That's him, all right."

Dunbar said, "Do you know if he was working for anybody?"

"I think he pestered half the people in town, but I don't know if anyone gave him a job."

The boss said, "Well, this is a hell of a mess. Just when we get going on this project, this bird comes along and fouls things up. Now we're going to have to take time to report it, and I suppose we might as well take the body to town while we're at it."

"I can do it," said Dunbar. "I can pack him on a horse. I can't go fast, but it won't take as long as the wagon. And I can go by myself. No need to take anyone else off of this job."

"Well, we can't leave him out here for the rest of the night, however much is left to it. We might as well put him in the barn and cover him with a canvas sheet. I don't feel sorry for him, but I don't like this . . . disruption."

The boss and Deke went to the bunkhouse. Tyler brought out a cart they used for feeding hay in the winter, and I held the lantern while he and Alan and Dunbar loaded the body and moved it. When we had it covered in the barn, I spoke to the two young men.

"Dunbar says he needs to study this, and I need to, as well. I think we'll compare notes here for a little while and meet the rest of you in the bunkhouse later."

"You bet," said Tyler. He and Alan took off.

With the door closed and the lantern hanging on a post, I turned my back on the body and said, "I don't think anyone will listen, but even if they do, I don't know how much it matters at this point."

"I agree." Dunbar cast a glance toward the cart. "I don't think this fellow came out on his own. I think someone has an idea I'm on his trail, and he's getting desperate."

"On his trail," I said.

"I don't think you should be very surprised, and you don't seem to be. But to get to the point, I came here looking for a person who caused the death of a *grisette* who worked out of a place called the Black Swan in Ogallala."

"The word you used—"

"*Grisette*? Sorry. A working girl. The type that some men seek out for their darker purposes."

"I understand."

"I did not have a name for my suspect. I was given to understand that he had changed his name and had come to this locale by way of Douglas and Fetterman."

"Oh, yes. There's a famous hog ranch there, which we've heard about."

"That's right. And so I ended up here. The trail being a bit faint, it took me to Kent Norland."

"Oh. I remember you asked him if he had worked in Nebraska."

"I did, but I didn't pursue it very much. By the time I met him, I did not think he was the perpetrator at the Black Swan. If he had been, he might well have said he hadn't worked in Nebraska. It seems as if he was a patron in Fetterman, as he was here, and he could have been in Ogallala, but he did not match the description or the pattern of the suspect there. He was secretive but not egocentric, or self-centered. He was insecure and weak, trying to dissociate himself from temptation, but not a person in control. A murderer of this nature—and I've followed a few like him, including one through North Platte—has supreme egotism. He is selfish. He has various ways of taking possession. I do not think our young friend was of that caliber, though I should be quick to add that one never knows for sure whether a given person would do thus-and-such a thing."

"This is ugly," I said. "I've heard stories of this sort before. Men commit crimes like this and go on their way and don't answer for them. It's not good."

"No, it's not. It's not good for anyone. A woman of

the streets in Ogallala or anywhere else matters, even if most of the average people don't care. In turn, their not caring makes it worse."

"I imagine you have a good idea of who it might be."

"I do, just as I imagine you do. But I don't have enough evidence. I have to guard against being too sure of myself and wanting to prove my own theory. I have a tendency to want to be always right, to have the correct knowledge even in small things that do not matter much. But in this case, my main obstacle is a lack of evidence."

"And you think he did in Kent Norland?"

"I do. Because he thought Norland might know something about his past and, as a lesser motive perhaps, because of the girl."

I flinched, but I stayed with it. "And you think he might have done the same to Ned Hacker, or had it done, to put the blame on him?"

"It could be that simple, but he may have been afraid that Hacker knew something as well. I think that deep down, he is afraid that Madeline knows something about his past, although I don't think she does. But he could have been afraid that Hacker heard something from her."

I took a deep breath to catch up. "It would be very satisfying to prove this older crime, but it seems one would have a better chance at proving these more recent ones first."

"Yes, but I'm still up against the same obstacle. Lack of evidence."

I hesitated for a moment and went ahead. "I can see that you're working on something important, and what I have to say is something I agreed not to share unless there was a very good reason."

He nodded. I appreciated that he did not prompt me.

"Do you remember the pendant that the madam of the Blue Diamond was wearing?"

"Of course. And you mentioned it afterwards."

"As you must have guessed, I had seen it before. Kent Norland showed it to me."

"No," he said. It was a rare moment for me to see him express real surprise.

"Yes. He told me that George Marven gave it to him. You remember who George Marven is?"

"Yes, the deputy mentioned him."

"Well, he talked Marven out of it, and he was planning to give it to Vivian. But he didn't get a chance to offer it to her, because she turned him down. I think he had it in his pocket the last time we saw him."

"Oh. It was part of his portable property, along with the watch. Now that is evidence. If the madam can tell us who gave it to her."

"And I don't think it was Ned Hacker. For one thing, I don't think he had a chance to go there in the meanwhile, although I know that if people want to have their secret meetings, they can find a way."

"Oh, no. I don't think it was him. But there I go again. I can't be too sure." He held me with his eyes. "We have to go to the Blue Diamond. You can identify it."

"Maybe I should ask the boss if I can go with you," I said, pointing with my thumb over my shoulder. "By the way, you do think that your main suspect hired him, don't you, and found him willing?"

"I think so. As you've mentioned, he has avoided me in every little way, as if he had some premonition. And even if he hasn't seen or heard us in conversation with Madeline, he knows we've been there and had an opportunity to talk to her."

I recalled that Madeline had also had a sense that Dunbar was an investigator. "Are you a Pinkerton man, or something like that?" I asked.

"I work on my own," he said.

"It doesn't matter. I don't know why I asked. What matters is the mission."

"For me, it's the woman in Ogallala. But as you say, we may be able to do something with these more recent deaths. I wonder where Deputy Caryl is. I have to see him about this other thing." He pointed with this thumb. "One thing at a time."

# 14

THE GREY LIGHT OF MORNING SHOWED THE SKELETAL building in place and unaffected by the events in the night. I had an awareness of the dead man under a canvas sheet in the barn while perhaps someone was waiting to hear from him. I imagined someone at least had supplied him with a horse.

The surface of the kitchen stove was hot when I held my open hand a couple of inches above it. The two skillets were warm, so I swabbed them with bacon grease and stirred the pancake batter again.

The wind was picking up with the dawn and was sweeping along the eaves. I imagined I would have a cold, dry gale in my face if I went to town with Dunbar. I thought about how I would phrase my request with the boss. My mind felt slow. I had not been able to go back to sleep, and I wondered how many of the others had been able to do so.

Men were making small talk by the heating stove in the main area of the bunkhouse. I recognized Deke's smooth voice and Dunbar's measured syllables. The front door opened, and Tyler came in, announcing that he had found the gun that we had not seen the night before. The intruder had not been wearing a holster, so we assumed he had carried it in his coat pocket and had dropped it when he ran. Tyler said it was a regular forty-five and he had left it with the body.

A quietness hovered over the breakfast table as the men made their way through the hotcakes, molasses, and coffee. I was still thinking of how to pose my question to the boss, even though it was not a difficult one, when hoofbeats sounded outside. I rose from my seat and took quick steps to the door. Cold air swirled when I opened it.

George Marven's hired man was wrapping reins around the hitching rail. He had come on horseback. He was wearing a wool cap with a beak and ear lugs, a lined canvas coat, and thick leather gloves. His pants billowed out where they were tucked into his boots.

His face was red, and he had not shaved for a few days. He raised his hand in greeting.

"Has something happened?" I asked. I stepped out and closed the door behind me.

"George needs to see you."

"Was he not able to come?"

"He's not in good shape. He's been shaken up."

"Did he take a fall?"

"No. Someone came to see him. Very early. When I came to do the chores, he took off."

"Is George by himself now?"

"No. Mrs. Hanley is there."

"How soon does he want to see me?"

"As soon as you can get there. You can ride back with me if you want."

I let out a tired breath. "Well, come in. I'll have to see about it."

The man stood by the stove and drank a cup of coffee as I explained the situation to Wes Galvin.

"I was thinking to ask if I could go with Dunbar, but this thing is taking me in the other direction."

The boss rocked his coffee mug back and forth with his large hand. "I'll say what I say when someone has to leave on personal business. Take as long as you need, but get back as soon as you can."

"Thanks."

"We're putting boards on today. It's going to be aggravating with the wind, but we have to keep going."

"Sure."

"You can leave as soon as you want. How are you going?"

"It looks like I'll have to take a horse."

"You'll have company going there. Do you feel all right about coming back by yourself?"

I did not know if he meant managing the horse or looking out for danger. "I guess I'll have to."

"Well, be careful."

Tyler went with Dunbar and me to the barn to get the horses ready for our separate trips. Dunbar said he would use his own horses, as he knew his packhorse well. Tyler brought Partner to me and stood by to watch as I brushed and saddled him. Dunbar came in with his two horses and told Tyler he could use his help when it came time to tie on the load. Marven's man came to the barn to wait for me, and I was glad to be ready to go before Tyler and Dunbar uncovered the dead freight.

I took Dunbar aside and told him I would look for him in town if I had something serious enough to take me there. He said he would not leave town before noon.

The wind came at us on a slant as we rode southeast to Marven's. The hired man was about my age, with a little more girth, and he did not push his horse beyond a fast walk. We arrived at Marven's place at midmorning.

I found George Marven sitting in front of a sheet-iron stove with a quilt over his lap. He was wearing a jacket that might have been made of camel hair, with a tan wool shirt beneath it and a turquoise-colored silk neck scarf. On his head he had a tan wool cap with a tuft, which, if it were plaid, I would have called a tam-o'-shanter. Mrs. Hanley stood about five feet away, and a table between them held a teapot and a cup.

Marven turned his pale face toward me and regarded me with his washed-out blue eyes. "Thank God you came, Edwin."

"What has happened?" I took off my hat.

"I've been roughed up. And it could have been much worse."

"How did it happen?"

"It came about as a result of things. All because I allowed that upstart to talk me out of the brooch."

I could see that he misinterpreted my question, but I assumed I would have an answer if I let him tell his story.

"Several days ago, a deputy came here to ask a number of questions about this young weed that had been struck down. Deputy named Caryl."

"I've met him."

"He told me that not only one but two of these ranch hands had been killed, and that the second one had the first one's watch on him."

"I knew that, also."

"The deputy said there was some doubt as to whether the second one killed the first one and took his watch. And since the second one turned up dead as well, the deputy thought there was still some danger at large—something big, he made it seem."

"I don't think he was wrong."

"Neither do I. And I didn't doubt him at the time. I thought things had become serious enough for me to tell him about the brooch."

"You did."

"Yes. And I can only assume that he used that knowledge in some of his questioning later." Marven took a slow, sad breath and blinked his eyes. "The next thing I know, a man is banging on my door in the middle of the night."

"Last night?"

"Yes. Actually, very early this morning. A tall man, about thirty-five or forty, well dressed for the kind of ruffian he turned out to be. He told me he was a store-keeper, and Vivian worked for him. He said he looked out for her, and he didn't like this young blade who was after her. He said the young man mingled with prostitutes." The last three words fell a syllable at a time.

"That may be."

"And then he became more belligerent. He told me I had to tell him everything I knew. I held out on him and told him I didn't know anything. And that's when he took me by the shoulders and put his hands on my throat and told me that, by God, either I told him what I knew or I would end up like the others." Marven faltered, cleared his throat, rubbed his nose with a handkerchief, and went on. "And so I told him about the brooch. I told him I had given it to the young swindler and I didn't know what happened to it after that."

"You don't know if Vivian had it."

Marven drew his shoulders together. "Well, I did find time to drive to town and ask her. She said she didn't know a thing about it."

"When was that?"

"Day before yesterday."

I registered that detail and said, "Now, back to your other story. What did you say when you told him about the pendant?"

"He asked me who else knew. I told him nobody. He said he thought I was lying but it didn't matter. I believe he would have choked me right there if Richard hadn't shown up and surprised him. He left in a hurry."

"I think he has plenty to worry about. And he could cause more harm yet."

Marven's head wavered. The area around his mouth moved, and he spoke. "I should never have let anyone have that brooch. I should have kept it stored away. It's bad luck. It has brought bad fortune to everyone who has had it."

"Everyone?"

"Well, Martha, Vivian's mother, and James, her father, and this young cowpoke named Norland—and now me, although it could have been worse."

"But you don't know who has it now."

"No, I don't. I don't think this ruffian has it, though."

A bumping sound at the door caused Mrs. Hanley to cross the room. She opened the door and let Richard in with an armload of firewood. After he left, I addressed Marven.

"What would you like me to do about this?"

Marven pursed his lips and relaxed them. "I think someone should report it. I'm in no condition to go all the way to town. But I'm afraid that some harm could come to Vivian, even though this man says he's been looking out for her."

"You can imagine how he looked, but I agree with you. It's a long ways for me to ride, but I think I ought to."

"I think you should, Edwin. This man is dangerous. He assaulted me."

I had more than one reason to take such a ride. I had an image of the diamond-and-emerald pendant resting on the smooth skin of the madam at the Blue Diamond, and I feared for her safety as well as Vivian's.

"I had better be going, George."

"Good, Edwin. And be careful. This isn't good work for old men."

I held my horse in place and put my foot in the stirrup. I pulled myself up, caught the other stirrup, and set out into the wind. I realized that George Marven had not thanked me for coming, and he found room to remind me of my age, but I had not told him about the last time I saw the pendant.

---

THE RIDE to Eminence was an ordeal that I knew I had to complete. I could not take the whole trip at a walk, or I would arrive too late, so I varied Partner's pace from a walk to a trot to a lope, back to a walk, and so on. My legs tired. Sometimes I held myself in the saddle with very little friction or slapping, while at other times I could not get my position right and had to slow to a walk and start over. The wind had also begun to throw sleet in my face, and by the time I reached town, snow was stinging my face and sticking to Partner's mane.

I found Dunbar with Deputy Caryl in the back of the barbershop with Dunbar's two horses tied outside. I assumed that the body beneath the sheet on the table was the same one that had been in the barn at the ranch. The deputy seemed buried in thought. He came out of his study to recognize me.

"I didn't know you were with him," he said, pointing with his thumb at Dunbar.

"I wasn't. I just came at a hard pace from George Marven's place." I went on to tell him the story that Marven told me.

The deputy held his small brown eyes on me. "Do you know where the pendant might be?"

"I know where I saw it last." Not to waste time, I said, "It was around the neck of the woman who runs the Blue Diamond."

He pushed his hat up as he scratched his head. "I don't know how soon I can go out there. This person didn't show up for work today, and we found her in the alley."

He drew back the sheet and showed the dusky face of Madeline Osborn, ashen now. Her eyes were closed, and her hair was disheveled.

I felt the shock in the pit of my stomach, and my throat was almost closed. "How did . . . where?"

"In the alley behind the hovel where she lived. It looked like she'd been there several hours. The marks on her throat are consistent with strangulation."

I noted the formal tone he was using even as I

struggled to accept the reality that this woman was no longer alive. "I had no idea. I thought this was the other one that came prowling at the ranch last night."

"He's over there." The deputy pointed at a canvas-covered form lying on the floor against the wall. "He knew her, didn't he?"

"Yes, but not in such a way that he would have done anything like that to her. If anything, he would have protected her—or tried."

The deputy covered the body on the table. "My estimate is that these things happened at around the same time. But I need to find out more. I need to see if there's any more evidence where she was found, and I need to ask people around there if they heard anything in the night."

I shook my head. "I don't know what to say. She wasn't all that bad."

The deputy stared at the sheet with a morose expression. "A lot of people who end up this way weren't all that bad."

"But this is wrong. It's . . . injustice."

He looked at me as if to say that it might be new to me but it was not to him.

"There's an obvious suspect," I said.

Dunbar spoke. "The mercantile is closed for the day, and he's not at his place of residence." From the way he said it, I guessed that he was repeating what he had been told.

"Then what are we waiting for?"

The deputy's small chin moved, and I thought he was making himself be patient with me. "I told you. I'm working on it."

Dunbar and I exchanged a glance and walked out into the alley.

"I can't believe this," I said. "But of course I have to. I guess what I'm trying to say is that I'm having a hard time accepting it. It's unreal at the same time that it's plain as day. And she had a sense that something like this might happen." I brushed the snow off the seat of my saddle. "I was thinking on the way in here that if I had told someone sooner about the pendant . . . but then again, I waited until I knew that you were working on an investigation. I don't know if we could have prevented some of this."

"We can't know. Things happened as they did, and we need to see what we can do from here."

I saw again the face of the woman lying on the table. "It was almost too much for me. And then to know that what's-his-name is lying on the floor in the same room." I felt myself settle as I let out a long breath. "He planned it well. Sent this one out in the country to get him out of the way and to kill two birds if he could."

"Seems like it."

"Poor woman. There were things about her that I found likeable." A stronger wave washed through me, and for a second I felt despair. "I don't know what I would have done if it had been someone closer to me. I don't know if I could get through it."

"I've checked on them," said Dunbar, "But if you'd like, we can go there now. Let me leave this packhorse in the livery stable first."

---

MRS. DEVILLE HAD the doors locked, but she let us in. Vivian was sitting at a table with Sophie. Both of them had eyes swollen from crying, but they were drawing pictures of flowers on a sheet of paper.

Mrs. Deville sat at her own table with a black-handled .38 in front of her.

Dunbar said, "The deputy has too many things to do, but we have an idea of where the man may have gone. It's a place called the Blue Diamond, a road ranch about five miles out."

I held Vivian's hand for a moment as our eyes met, and then I followed Dunbar to the door. Mrs. Deville locked it behind us as the sound of the bell faded.

---

A LIGHT SNOW was blowing as we took the trail northeast. When we had town behind us, Dunbar spoke.

"I didn't say this in town because I didn't want to shout in the wind, but I had a few words with the man in the livery stable. He said our man rented two horses yesterday afternoon and brought one back in the middle of the morning today. He wanted two more to go out again. The livery man asked him where the other horse was, and he said the man must have gotten lost and he and his hired man were going out to look for him and the horse. I take the hired man to be the clerk. Give them time to get a few items together, and they have about a two-hour start on us. I don't think they'll travel very fast, so if we lope a mile at a time, we should be able to close some of the distance on them."

Off we went, with me bouncing and slapping in the saddle from time to time but also holding my seat and riding with the rhythm of the horse. Partner was breathing hard, but we covered the ground.

In less than an hour, we arrived at the Blue Diamond. It had not changed in appearance since our last visit a few days earlier, but it had an isolated atmosphere and seemed drawn into itself in the falling snow. We tied our horses and knocked on the door as before. Dunbar took off his gloves and put them away.

The latch clacked, and the door opened. Cage Whitman blocked the doorway. He was wearing a tobacco-colored pullover sweater with a high neck, which, with the darkness of his bowler hat, brought out his heavy brows and shadowed eyes. He dragged his hand across the bottom of his nose and rested it near the butt of his pistol.

"What do you want?" His eyes traveled back and forth and settled on Dunbar.

"We're looking for someone."

"Your sniveler?"

"Someone else I think you know. Raymond Fell."

"What of him?"

"He comes to this place, doesn't he?"

"That's none of your business."

"Did you know him in Fetterman?"

"That's nonc of your concern, either."

"A little bit better kind of patron?"

"Most of what I saw there was your common cowhands, railroad workers, and soldiers. I don't know what you're getting at."

"We're looking for him today, and you'd be better off if you didn't try to protect him."

"I don't let someone like you tell me what to do, bub."

"Has he been here today?"

"Oh, get out!" Whitman spit at Dunbar, not a gob but more than a few drops.

Dunbar grabbed him by the sweater and dragged him across the threshold. He slammed him up against the wall, released him, and punched him with a right and a left. Whitman sagged, and Dunbar pulled the pistol from his holster.

"I'll leave this inside," he said.

I followed Dunbar into the entryway and on into the parlor. Two women gasped and gave small shrieks as they stood by the far end of the sofa. They were dressed in housecoats, and their hair was bedraggled, but I recognized them as Maisie and Peg. Their madam was lying on the couch.

Her left arm was hanging over the edge of the sofa. Her blond hair was in disarray, and the front of her blue dress was torn. Her chest was bare. A tiny gold chain lay by itself on the floor near her left hand.

"Has Raymond Fell been here?" asked Dunbar.

Florence Mallow moved her head but did not speak. Peg had her hands over her mouth, and Maisie was pulling her housecoat tight around herself.

"Did he take the jewel?" I asked.

Still no one answered.

"Look," said Dunbar. "This is no time to be coy. A woman who has been in your line of work has been murdered in town. Left in the alley. And he is on the run. When was he here?"

Maisie said, "About an hour ago."

"He came for the pendant, didn't he?" I asked. "The jewel."

Maisie nodded.

Dunbar spoke. "Did he have a creepy-looking fellow with him?"

Peg said, "He was holding the horses."

"Did you see which way they went?" I asked.

They both shook their heads.

Dunbar laid Whitman's pistol on the other end of the sofa. "This is the doorman's," he said.

I took off my hat. "I'm sorry for what happened to your boss lady."

"She'll be all right," said Maisie. "He was rough on her, and I think it gave her a shock."

"I wish her the best," said Dunbar. He touched his hat, and I followed him out the door.

Outside, Cage Whitman was nowhere to be seen. Footprints in the snow led around to the back of the building.

"No time to lose," said Dunbar.

We began to ride a circle around the roadhouse, and Dunbar picked up a trail leading to the southeast. He pointed out the crescents in the thin snow.

"Hard to tell what someone else is thinking," he said. "This might be his idea of an unexpected direction. Do you know of a town this way?"

"Just rangeland." I pictured the trail as if I was looking at a map. A dotted line was making the third side of a diamond from George Marven's up to the Hook ranch to town and now down from here. I did not think the fugitives would close the diamond but would keep going southeast if they could in the general direction of Nebraska.

"Well, it's time to ride again."

With a rustle of saddle leather and a drumming of hooves, we were off again. I felt the wind at my back on the right side, and the snowflakes did not fly straight in my face.

The snowfall remained light, and the clouds were high, but the landscape closed off at about two miles all the way around. The country was wide open, with no bluffs or buttes in view. The land rose in low swells and fell away in broad stretches. No trees or buildings appeared. I saw a windmill straight east, and I thought that sooner or later, we would see a fence.

We rode for about five miles. The country was still a wide expanse ahead when Dunbar drew rein at the crest of a low hill and I stopped with him. A mile ahead, on a plain that was grey in the strained light, small figures were visible.

As I peered, I began to make out the situation. A man was leading a horse. Ahead of him, to my left, a man was walking fast. Ahead of him, a horse danced, stopping for several seconds and then trotting on.

Dunbar held a small pair of binoculars to his eyes. "It's Fell. The other one is leading a horse, and he's limping. My guess is that he got thrown, and one way or the other, Fell lost hold of his."

"One of them should get on that horse and go catch the other," I said.

"They may not know how to do that."

I thought, even I had done that much. But I was not a storekeeper, and I was glad I was not the one on foot in the elements.

Dunbar said, "I think we should approach them, but not fast. Even if they both get mounted, I think we can catch them."

We rode down the slope at a fast walk. The procession out on the flat continued until someone must have seen us.

By now it was more evident which one was Fell. He moved as in a motion picture, turning and stalking back toward his partner, who had stopped with the horse. They began to move in small motions, and it appeared that they were arguing over the horse.

Dunbar and I kept riding. When we had come within half a mile, the scene changed. Fell raised his arm, and Herman staggered as I heard a loud *pop!* Herman slumped to the ground, and Fell yanked on the reins of the horse.

The animal was moving away, circling with its hind end, as Fell pulled on the reins and moved toward it with his hand raised. He reached for the bridle, reached for the saddle horn, stumbled, but held onto the reins. At last he held the horse still and had the reins in place.

Dunbar and I were trotting now. Fell had lost his hat. He looked over his shoulder and showed his nose in profile as he clawed at the rear of the saddle with his right hand and held the reins and saddle horn in his left. He was tall enough, and the stirrup was adjusted long enough, that he was able to put his foot in the stirrup without much trouble. The horse moved, and Fell hopped on his right foot until he pulled himself up and clambered on.

The horse took off at a fast walk, jiggled the rider with a trot, and broke into a lope. It was heading northwest now, but I thought Fell would ride it wherever it went. He was hanging onto the saddle horn and had both reins in hand.

The loose horse turned and watched with its reins trailing.

Dunbar and I followed the man, but we did not gain on him by very much. The grass and sagebrush under a light layer of snow flowed by. Partner zigzagged to avoid a bush, and I had to grab the pommel.

The land began to slope downward in the direction we were heading. The area ahead came into view as we rode toward it, and at last I saw what I had expected.

A barbed-wire fence, with the dark strands like hairline against the background, ran from west to east ahead of us. Approaching it at an angle, Fell's horse followed it to the right. We cut off a little of the distance by following on a diagonal.

The horse ahead had slowed from the speed when it first took off, and it ran at a steady lope with Fell clutching the saddle horn. As we gained, the horse began to slow more and more, and I saw the reason. Another fence ran north and south, a quarter of a mile ahead, and the ground sloped away into a draw beyond it.

"Don't get too close," said Dunbar. "He might shoot." He began to veer to the right, just as if he was going to keep a steer from going that way.

Fell's horse came bunching to a stop in the corner of the two fences. I drew up about forty yards behind him, and Dunbar had turned and blocked his escape on the right. We each let our horses move forward a few inches at a time.

Silence held until Dunbar called out, "Fell!"

"What the hell do you want?" Fell had turned to face us. He was less than thirty yards away. With his hat gone, his hair was matted against his head. His face was clear, and his dark eyes resembled those of a crow. I could see the recognition that what he had feared had come for him.

"You should give yourself up. For the death of Kent Norland. And for the death of Anna England."

The name was unfamiliar to me, and it sounded strange as it was called out in the damp, chilly air in the middle of nowhere, in a spot where two fences came together and three men faced off. But the name struck a difference on Fell's face. His features stiffened, and his dark eyes stared. He looked at each of us, as if he could see his doom and still hoped to escape it.

He turned his horse to the right and to the left, and Dunbar and I both held still. Fell ran his horse five yards each way, but the horse stopped short of the fence on the east and the gully beyond it. Fell ran the horse back and forth, stopped again, and faced Dunbar. He had his coat opened. He took out a small pistol, raised it, and fired a shot. Dunbar's horse lurched to the side as the bullet went by, but Dunbar held on and came up with his own pistol. He aimed but did not fire. I could tell he was not going to take a bad shot. This was his mission, and he was not going to ruin it.

Fell's horse did not stand still. He let it run again in my direction, then made a wide turn around and ran it toward the fence. Ten yards to the right of the corner, the fence was lower where it went down through the edge of the draw and came up. Fell headed full tilt for the low spot and kicked the horse.

The horse was a dark bay. Its mane fluttered and its tail streamed as Fell's black coat lifted and trailed. The horse tripped on the top wire, bunched, and turned. It landed in a heap on its front shoulder with a loud thud. Fell traveled over the horse and hit the earth with a cracking sound that made me shake.

He did not move as the horse scrambled to its feet and trotted away with the stirrups swinging. He did not move as Dunbar and I rode up to the fence and stopped.

Dunbar said, "He falls like Lucifer. Never to hope again."

A calm was taking over. "This is not tragedy," I said.

"No, it's not. The ancient rules spell it out. The tragic figure has to have something good in him. A bad person meeting up with justice is a good outcome, but there is no tragic loss."

His manner of speaking reminded me of the day he talked about the ghost ships. As we gazed across the fence, I felt that he could have killed a rattlesnake next to his face as he lay in his bedroll on the ground, and as soon as the danger was over, he could have explained original sin.

He seemed to have an awareness of being so ready to show his knowledge. He made a squeaking sound in the corner of his mouth. "Enough of philosophy. We need to get these horses and bodies back to town. There's got to be a gate in this fence somewhere."

# 15

SNOW HAD BEGUN TO PILE UP IN SMALL DRIFTS WHEN we rode into town with the two horses in tow. We stopped in front of the hotel, where light spilled out of the windows. I heaved myself out of the saddle, found my legs, and went in to ask for Deputy Caryl.

I gave him a brief summary of what had happened.

"And so you have them here?" he said.

"Right outside."

"At least we don't have to go out and bring 'em in. But I don't know where I'm going to put two more."

"We might be able to make space in the back room of the mercantile."

"That's an idea. I'll send for the barber to meet us there in the alley."

The deputy walked in front of us with his hands in his coat pockets. He led us to the back of the store and stood in the lee of a shed. Still in his calm voice, he said, "I should have done this in better light. I need to see if I can find a set of keys on him."

Dunbar said, "They're in the bag on the back of the saddle. They fell out when we were loading him."

I remembered picking up the keys and wondering if Fell had a thought for coming back for his material interests.

Inside the back room, the deputy lit a match and found a lamp. He lit it and a second one. We were clearing off a work table when the barber arrived. He was wearing a long white coat like a duster and a grey wool hat.

"Two of 'em, eh?"

I said to the deputy, "We might want to look over the owner first. We didn't find the jewel. We searched his pockets to make sure it wouldn't fall out like the keys did."

We laid Fell on the table. As we brought Herman in to lie on the floor, the deputy went through Fell's pockets. When he was done, he shook his head.

"He had a penknife and some money," I said. "We put those along with his watch in the bag that had his name on it."

Dunbar brought the satchel, and the deputy emptied it on the table. He set the clothes aside, opened and closed the cigarette case with the stitched diamond pattern, and poked through the comb, brush, razor, cuff links, and watch and chain. He shook his head again.

"We'll look at the other bag, just to be sure."

"The clerk's pockets are empty, too," I said. "His things are in the bag."

The second bag was like the first, with clothes, toiletries, and personal effects, but no jewelry except a round, black onyx ring with a gold border.

The deputy said, "I wonder where else he might have it, if he did."

"He took it from the madam," I said. "It was the one thing he would want to hoard."

The deputy twisted his mouth. "Maybe he threw it away. Get rid of the evidence."

"It was his nature to hang onto things. He kept his keys, even though he had burned his bridges here."

Dunbar said, "This fellow was quite the possessor. I think he would want to keep control of it. I wouldn't be surprised if he had it inside him."

"Inside?" said the deputy.

"Yes." Dunbar took on his academic tone. "I imagine you know that people smuggle or hide things that way. Small items of value, like smooth stones—pearls, rubies, or an emerald by itself. Sometimes they take them in from one end or push them in from the other. Sometimes they use other conveyances, like children or animals."

The barber said, "Like the Sherlock Holmes story of the blue carbuncle."

Dunbar smiled. "That's been a popular story. I imagine it's been in the magazines in half the barbershops in the country. The technique, of course, is an old one for smugglers both male and female."

The barber's face lit up. "Do you think he swallowed it?"

"He could have. A coroner could find out."

The barber shifted from side to side with his hands in his coat pockets. "Bottles of rubbing alcohol here. Right next to the liniment and rat poison. I brought a couple of instruments with me."

"I don't think we need to watch," I said. "We could go to the café and see if anyone is there."

"Good idea," said Dunbar. "We can leave the two horses at the livery stable. It's just a little out of our way."

---

LIGHT WAS SHOWING in the café window. We tied our horses and knocked on the door. Mrs. Deville let us in. Vivian was sitting at a table, and Sophie was sleeping on two chairs with a coat draped over her. We took off our hats and stood in the warm, lit room.

Mrs. Deville had a steady look in her dark eyes. "We heard the news that those two had been brought in."

"That's right," said Dunbar.

"We decided to wait here. I imagine you could use a cup of coffee and something to eat."

"I think we have time," he said.

Vivian rose from her chair and took my hand. "I was so worried for both of you."

I looked into her blue eyes, so bright and shiny by nature but now so sad. "I know this has been very difficult, but I think the danger has passed."

She blinked away a tear. "I hope so. Now, I need to help Medora."

Dunbar and I sat at a table, and within a few minutes we each had a warm bowl of stew in front of us. Mrs. Deville and Vivian sat down with us.

Dunbar said, "We need to go back to where the deputy and the barber are taking care of things. But while we're here, I wouldn't mind asking a couple of questions."

"Regarding?" said Mrs. Deville.

Dunbar motioned with his head toward the

kitchen. "Regarding our friend who worked here. I don't mean to sound cold. Rye and I both found her likeable. But there are a couple of things I would like to know in order to have a better understanding of . . . what may have happened before."

Mrs. Deville's eyes focused on him. "Go ahead."

"In the course of conversation, did she talk to either of you about her past?"

"She talked to Vivian more than she did to me. If she said anything personal to me, it was to thank me for helping her with her circumstances."

We all gave our attention to Vivian.

Her voice was shaking as she began. "She talked in general terms about her past. She said she had done work like this, cleaning and scrubbing, and work less reputable. She didn't have to speak in detail. I understood."

Dunbar nodded. "Did she talk about how she came to have the care of this child, or how she knew the child's mother?"

"A little. She said she knew Sophie's mother—" Vivian lowered her voice as she glanced at the sleeping girl. "She said she knew the child's mother in Cheyenne. They did similar work there."

Dunbar said, "She told us she had worked in Cheyenne, also."

"They became friends, and they made an agreement that if anything ever happened to . . . the mother, then Madeline would take care of the child. I believe the mother had it in her papers that Madeline was to have custody."

"And they left Cheyenne."

"Yes. Their work went bad there, as she put it, and

they went their separate ways. Madeline ended up here, and the girl's mother went to Ogallala."

I felt a catch in my throat.

"Ogallala?" said Dunbar.

"Yes, in Nebraska."

"I know where it is. Excuse me. I just wanted to make sure." Dunbar was not showing any interest in his food.

"That was it. That was where she died. And that was how the little girl came to live here with Madeline."

"And do you have an idea of how long ago this was?"

"Between two and three years, I think. She wasn't in Ogallala for very long."

"Fell has been here about two years," I said.

"The time fits," said Dunbar. Addressing Vivian again, he said, "Did Madeline ever mention the mother's name?"

"Anna. She said her friend's name was Anna."

I was not surprised, but I felt a tightness in my chest and a shortness of breath all the same. I said to Dunbar, "Is that the name—"

"Yes. I mentioned it to Fell before he went headlong." Dunbar shifted his attention and spoke to Mrs. Deville and Vivian, although Mrs. Deville did not seem to be hearing the story for the first time. "I have been on the trail of a person who strangled a woman named Anna England in Ogallala, Nebraska. He met her in a place called the Black Swan. He had his way with her and left her dead. I tracked him to Fetterman, from information that I had, but I did not know his name. Things got crossed up, because Kent Norland had been at Fetterman as well and may have been in Ogallala, and they both ended up here."

Vivian was following the story with close attention.

Our last conversation with Madeline led me to believe that Fell suspected that Kent Norland had some suspicion of him. He may even have thought that he was following him. Fell patronized Madeline, in addition to the usual reason, with the motive of finding out if Norland ever said anything about him to her. Which he didn't. But Fell had his fears, and he disliked Norland for reasons of petty jealousy. So he killed him, took some personal items, and planted the watch on Ned Hacker, who may have brought some of his fate upon himself by snooping around and by antagonizing Fell in general. All this time, Fell was afraid that Madeline knew too much, so either he or Herman strangled her."

I said, "But you don't think Madeline knew how Anna England came to die."

"In terms of the identity of her killer, no. And neither Norland, if he had ever been to Ogallala, nor Fell ever mentioned the town to her. If she had known Fell had been there, she would have kept a great distance away from him. She might have gone to another town or city."

I pondered. "So she and the little girl walked past his store and never knew."

"That's right. And I would guess that he did not have an idea, either." Dunbar straightened up, and his voice quickened. "Of course, I don't know for sure, either. Not dead certain. But I am convinced."

He returned to eating his stew, and the table went quiet. I stole a look at him. When I had first met him, less than a month earlier, he had presented himself as a cowpuncher who had read Shakespeare, graveyard poetry, and sad novels. But it was evident that he had seen and learned a great deal about life. He had come to know some of the darkest aspects of human nature at first hand. On a couple of earlier occasions, I had recognized that a younger person might have wisdom and insight that an older person might not arrive at. Now as I saw him eating his lukewarm stew, I realized that the world was in the hands of many people and that those of us who were growing older could only hope that those coming up had judgment and principle.

---

UNDER THE TWO lamps in the back room of the mercantile, another work table had been cleared off, and both bodies were covered with sheets. On the sheet that covered Raymond Fell, a small diamond and an emerald smaller than my small fingernail were shining in the light.

The barber wore a close-mouthed smile. When Dunbar and I had both observed the pendant and stepped back, the barber spoke in a cheerful tone. "I found it as you suggested, where he swallowed it. I cleaned it off with alcohol."

The deputy said, "I'll keep it for evidence until I write my report, but I don't think anything will go to court. As I see it, with these two on ice, the case is closed. Who should have the jewel when I'm done?"

Dunbar deferred to me.

"I would say George Marven. He let Kent Norland have it, but he wished he hadn't, and it never became the proper property of anyone else."

The deputy nodded. "I'll make a note of it."

I said, "I think he'll want it back, though I also think he has a superstition about it, as if it has brought a bad fate to anyone who has had it."

Dunbar said, "So far, but in various degrees. He and the madam both lived through it. The pendant still has its value, and if some future owner doesn't know the history, it might outlive its unlucky charm." He smiled. "Superstition exists for people who believe in it or who know that this thing or that is supposed to be unlucky—like throwing your hat on a bed. Or lucky, like whether you hang a horseshoe up or down."

"Then you're not superstitious?" I said.

"I wouldn't say that, not as an absolute statement. But I'm not afraid of having thirteen trusses or a black cat to guard the grain."

The barber said, "Well, I don't believe in those things, either, but there are some that might say it brought bad luck to this fellow."

"Let them believe what they will," said Dunbar. "I think he made his own fate."

I thought the best thing he did was try to jump that fence, but I realized he had made his fate much earlier.

---

FROST WAS SHOWING on the tar paper roof and board sides of the shed when Tyler brought the wagon around to the bunkhouse door. As he was going to ride into town with me in the wagon, he stayed in the seat. Alan and Deke had their bags ready, and Dunbar was tightening the lashes on his buckskin packhorse. The boss had paid the three workers after breakfast, so now it was time for the short goodbye.

He shook hands and said so long to the three who were leaving.

We arrived in town in midmorning and stopped in front of the post office. I let myself down with care, as I was still sore from all the riding I had done a few days earlier. Deke and Alan climbed down from the wagon and took their belongings, and we had our second little round of farewell. Dunbar rode to the café while I went in for the mail. Outside, I asked Tyler if he would like to go with me to the café, and he said yes.

When we parked the wagon by Dunbar's horses and went into the café, I was surprised to see Mrs. Deville's Gladstone bag sitting on a table. Her grey cap and traveling coat lay next to it, along with her black gloves.

Sophie was sitting at the next table, drawing with a pencil on a sheet of paper. She was wearing a clean set of clothes, and her thick hair was held in place with a pair of curved combs. Vivian stood by with a white apron over her light blue dress. Mrs. Deville was talking to Dunbar.

"Is someone leaving?" I asked.

Vivian smiled, and her eyes were shining. "Medora is turning the business over to me."

"Indeed?" I said. "Are you ready for that?"

"I think so. We have the agreement signed, and I have an address for sending the payments."

I reflected. The day was Monday. The northbound stage went through in the forenoon on Mondays and Wednesdays. Mrs. Deville had arrived on the southbound, later in the day on a Saturday. From the circumstances, I did not think she would be leaving with Dunbar and his horses.

Dunbar's voice was cheerful. "I'm going to walk

Mrs. Deville to the station, or stage stop. Care to go along?"

"I suppose I could." I met Vivian's eyes.

"We'll stay here," she said. "We've already said goodbye."

I turned to Tyler. He had taken off his black hat and stood at ease. "I'll stay here and keep an eye on the wagon and horses."

It looked as if he was taking the opportunity to watch from inside, in company. "Good enough," I said.

Dunbar carried the Gladstone bag and walked on the street side. I walked behind the two of them.

A small group of people had gathered outside the hotel to see the stagecoach come in. Thad Coulter was among them, leaning on his tall cane. He doffed his hat and said, "The lady leaves."

Mrs. Deville smiled at him.

The stagecoach came in with a rattle of running gear and a rumble of hooves. The driver pulled it to a stop and called out, "Eminence!" He climbed down and opened the door. No one stepped out.

He turned and spoke to Mrs. Deville. "Only one other passenger. You can take your bag inside with you."

Dunbar swept off his hat, handed her up into the coach, and lifted her bag. The driver closed the door.

I assumed Dunbar and Mrs. Deville had said their goodbyes earlier as well.

The small crowd dispersed as the stagecoach rolled away. Dunbar and I began walking toward the café.

When we were alone, I said, "This is just an old man speaking to a young man, and excuse me if I am being too forward, but how could you let her get away?"

"Oh, that's not quite it," he said. "I still have things to do, but those things won't keep me from seeing her again. I hope."

I thought I understood. There was a difference between a person having a mission and assuming that he had plenty of life ahead.

At the café, Dunbar stepped inside long enough to say goodbye to Tyler and Vivian and Sophie.

"I'll see you off," I said.

Outside, he gave me his right hand. I saw the mark in his palm for a second.

"So long, Rye. It's been good to know you."

"And goodbye to you, Dunbar. It's been more than a pleasure. Thanks for all you've done."

He led his horses into the street and stopped, with the roan half a length ahead of the buckskin and turned away at the hip. With his left hand holding the reins and saddle horn and his right hand holding the lead rope out of the way, he stepped up into the saddle and swung his leg over. He touched his hat as he turned the blue roan and set off.

He did not ride through town. Rather, he rode east to the end of the street and turned north without looking back. I wandered that way and watched. He crossed the trail that led northeast to the Blue Diamond, and he kept riding straight north. Patches of snow remained from a few days earlier, and his horses raised little puffs that carried on the breeze.

---

Late fall has come around twice more since Dunbar left. The cold wind blows across the plain, and

I look upward to the sound of geese as I gather firewood.

Tyler and I are still working at the Hook ranch. We are the two employees who stay year-round. Riders come and go, some with tall tales and some with few words. I ride a horse at least once a week in good weather.

Wes Galvin put a tin roof on the shed after one year of tar paper. He has a black cat with white on its nose and chest, and he receives a "heart and hand" matrimonial paper in the mail. He spends some evenings by the stove, writing letters with a short pencil in his large hand, before he copies them in ink.

Vivian has the café, and she has undertaken the care of Sophie, who lives with her at the boardinghouse. Alan works in the kitchen and seems content with his position. Tyler is always ready to ride into town with me and to stop at the café. Thad Coulter drops by on his almost daily rounds, hobbling past the empty mercantile store on his way. Sometimes I walk past it myself, and once in a while I peer in to see the empty space where the stuffed hawk had its perch.

I also go the barbershop, where Jake likes to remind me of how he found the pendant. He tells me, as I imagine he tells others, that George Marven says he threw the jewel into the North Platte River near Orin Junction. He may have.

I find time to visit with Mrs. Williams at the boardinghouse. I have told her that although there may be snow on the roof, there is fire in the chimney, and like Dunbar, I admit that I heard the phrase elsewhere. She and I have plenty to talk about. I believe we both see the time ahead as one in which we have to manage our life energy as well as our hearth fires.

Sometimes, as when I think of Madeline, I feel guilty for living longer when other people's lives are cut short. As I have thought of things, I have arrived at the idea that many people, including the non-guilty, cannot escape the past. I also realize, more than before, that some people cause a great deal of harm with no right to cause any of it.

I am thankful that Dunbar did what he could. I hope he finds an opportunity to spend time with Mrs. Deville, away from trouble, if he has not already done so. But I am also glad that he said he still had things to do.

## A LOOK AT:

RIDERS OF THE SKULL

**Jord Blaine never set out to make enemies. He just refused to make the right ones.**

Blaine has no quarrel with the Skull outfit… until the foreman orders his men to ride down a group of Cajun homesteaders trying to scratch a living from the Wyoming plains. Blaine refuses. Twice. His firmness costs him his job and earns him something worse: an enemy who doesn't let insults go unanswered.

He finds new work, rides into the mountains with a hunting party, and figures the trouble is behind him. Then a shot rings out that was never meant for the elk. The Skull's reach is longer than he thought, and young Jimmy Baker—the decent kid Blaine worked alongside all summer—is now riding for the very men hunting him down.

Blaine didn't want a fight. But the Skull doesn't leave a man the choice.

***AVAILABLE MAY 2026***

# THANK YOU

Thank you for taking the time to read *Diamonds and Doom*. If you enjoyed it, please consider telling your friends or posting a short review. Word of mouth is an author's best friend and much appreciated.

Thank you.
*John D. Nesbitt*

# ABOUT THE AUTHOR

John D. Nesbitt is the author of more than fifty books, including traditional Westerns, crossover Western mysteries, contemporary Western fiction, retro/noir fiction, nonfiction, and poetry. He has won the Western Writers of America Spur Award four times—twice for paperback novel, once for short story, and once for poem. He has won the Western Fictioneers Peacemaker Award twice—once for novel and once for short story. He has been a finalist for the Spur Award twice, the Peacemaker nine times, and the Will Rogers Medallion Award nine times. He has also received two creative writing fellowships with the Wyoming Arts Council—once for fiction, once for nonfiction—and he has won the fiction award four times with the Wyoming State Historical Society. Visit his website at johndnesbitt.com.

www.ingramcontent.com/pod-product-compliance
Lightning Source LLC
La Vergne TN
LVHW040217110826
845146LV00005B/1318

* 9 7 9 8 8 9 5 6 7 3 7 4 4 *